Mom's Old Testament Bible Stories

Mom's Old Testament Bible Stories

HEROES AND SCOUNDRELS

Shirley Fillmore Ness

authorHOUSE®

AuthorHouse™
1663 Liberty Drive
Bloomington, IN 47403
www.authorhouse.com
Phone: 1-800-839-8640

First published by AuthorHouse   11/16/2009

ISBN: 978-1-4490-5041-2 (e)
ISBN: 978-1-4490-5040-5 (sc)
ISBN: 978-1-4490-5039-9 (hc)

Library of Congress Control Number: 2009912187

Printed in the United States of America
Bloomington, Indiana

This book is printed on acid-free paper.

This book is dedicated to my four kids:
Dr. Kathy Buxie, PHD statistics
Rev. Dave Ness, Master of Divinity
Dr. Bill Ness, PHD English Literature
Julie Jamison, Master of Computers

With thanks for all the times they listened to
these stories while they were drying dishes when
they were young. We had a LOT of dishes.

and

to all the young people and children who will
read or have these stories read to them.

Perhaps you will find a Hero to follow. I hope that
you get the picture of what God did in the Old
Testament trying to bring people back to himself.

It is His world. He created it. He loves it and
He loves YOU.
God Bless

Shirley Fillmore Ness

Thank you to: David for editing

Pictures are by:
Rebekah, age 10
and
Steven, age 8

Stories and quotes are from the King James and NIV Bibles.

Foreword

As a child, my mother told each of her children all of the stories of the Bible, individually, usually while she was washing dishes and we were drying them. These stories planted within each one of us a great respect and love for the Bible. Told in her own words, with great emotion, I received Mom's Bible stories as one of the greatest gifts ever given to me. Recently, I asked her to write down some of these stories in much the same way she told them to us when we were children. If you want to read or tell these stories to your own children or grandchildren, it will be a blessing to them throughout their days. (Note: I love the way the Bible tells the whole story, not just the nice parts, but younger children may not yet be ready for all the parts of these stories. Use wisdom and just skip over any sections for which you feel they're not ready.)

Dave Ness

Dave has been a pastor of the Church of the Nazarene for many years. He planted the church in Cordova, Alaska, and pastored in Carson, and Longview, Washington for 22 years. He resigned his church 3 years ago to start "Servant Connection" working with pastors all over the Kelso- Longview area in Washington. It is a nonprofit ministry devoted to the spiritual transformation of America. Dave has written a daily devotional book called "Serving God", and has a web cite: "PrayingforAmerica.org" He, his wife, Joy, and their two children live in Longview, Washington.

Introduction

I grew up in Mitchell, South Dakota where my father was the YMCA secretary and my mother was YWCA secretary all my growing up years. At home, my mother told us Bible stories, so interestingly that I began to read the Bible for myself at an early age. I found the Old Testament stories fascinating. They explained how others had dealt, both good ways and bad, with some of the problems that I was having growing up. These are the heroes from our culture. The greatest art and music of the past is based on them. Our kids need to know about them.

My husband, Maynard, and I raised four children on our farm about 10 miles north of Fulton, SD. With 6 of us in the family, we had a lot of dirty dishes. My kids hated to dry dishes, so I started using that time to tell them Bible stories. It kept them interested and willing to help. My son later said that he never heard a Bible story in church that he hadn't first heard at home.

I have taught Sunday School classes to children, quizzing to teens, and adult Sunday school class for 60 years. I love the Bible. It has been a joy trying to put it into language our kids will understand, empathize with, and hopefully, find a hero they can learn from and copy, as it fits their own lives.

Kids need heroes. They are finding too many of them who lead them astray. Bible heroes lead them to a life that is useful, loving, and Godly. Christian young people need to know about these Jewish Heroes who kept the faith, so that God could bring Jesus into the world. Jewish young people need to know their own history. All of us need heroes.

Mom's Old Testament Bible Stories
Heroes And Scoundrels

A hero is someone worthy of trying to copy, someone who can do things you thought you could never do, someone who does wonderful things in life. When people have physical abilities, mental abilities, spiritual abilities above and beyond what most of us can accomplish, we tend to make them our heroes. It is good to have heroes who inspire us to be more than we thought we could ever be. We see many of them in the Bible. We are going to look at some of them in this book. I hope you enjoy seeing them as I do.

The first Hero of all in the Bible is GOD. We start out with Him because who else could ever look out on total darkness and envision a world with stars, galaxies of stars, suns, moons, and an earth with creatures on it?! And if you could imagine it, how could anyone build it? Yet, God did. He only had to speak it into existence. So who is this God with such power?

The entire Bible is trying to show us this God. In the Old Testament, He is the creator God. He does not have a body like we do. God is Spirit. God is three in One, much like we are. We have a spirit, mind and body. God is the Father, Son, and Holy Spirit. He has always been. He will always be!

God is LOVE. (I didn't say that love is God.) God is Love! Don't get it confused. God is Holy Love. Love that loves unconditionally, not because the loved one is worthy, but because the lover is worthy, and has ability to love so much. Love that does whatever is best for the one who is loved, even if it hurts the lover. Love, like what is described in I Corinthians 13.

1

Who could build a universe, lose it to the enemy He had created, and find a way to win it back that cost Him his own human life? But God did! All other religions have a god who must be found and appeased. Our God is the only one who came to His creation in love and saved it.

WHAT A HERO!!

Genesis
Creation

Rebekah

In the beginning, God. God was always there. Before anything else, there was God. He will always be.

In the beginning, God created the heavens and the earth. We didn't create Him. He created our world, our universe, all the animals--us.

We don't know when it all began, but one day, God looked out and decided to make something. Everywhere He looked there was deep, dark space, darkness, water everywhere.

God said, "Let there be light", and there was light. Everywhere God is, there is light, so when God gave it His attention, there was light.

God was just getting started. He made a firmament--the sky with all its stars and galaxies; dividing the waters; creating the earth; dividing the water on the earth; and calling up the dry land.

God knew that the things He would be creating would need food, so He made grass to grow, trees to produce fruit, each with its seed in itself so it could produce more trees; and grass.

On the fourth day, God created the sun, moon and stars, the seasons, day and night. God said that it was good.

Now everything was in place to create animals, so He started in the ocean, creating fish, whales, etc., then moved to dry land and created cattle, creeping things, birds and every beast of the earth. Not all the varieties that we have today, but original ones of each kind. God looked at it and said that it was good.

God had one main idea: to make a man who would talk with Him, walk with Him, depend on Him, be His friend, and love and serve Him. So, on the sixth day, God formed a man in His own image--a spirit and mind, in a body made of dirt.

Now, we know that God is Spirit. He doesn't have a body, but He gave man a body to live in while he is on earth. He formed man out of the dust of the earth. Then He breathed into man's nostrils the "Breath of Life," and man became a living soul! God looked at all He had created and said that it was "very good!"

God was satisfied with his creation. It had taken Him six days to do it. But we know that the Bible says that a thousand years is like a day to God, so we really have no idea how long it took. God rested on the seventh day from His labor, and told man to rest on the seventh day, too. God wasn't tired, but He knew that man needed that day of rest.

God's universe is mathematically correct in every way, and everything works together in harmony. Every body has its own special system and reproductive way so the entire universe will continue as God planned it, unless something messes it up.

God's creative genius shows in all the systems, in everything: birds fly, trees produce fruit, fish have gills and swim, people walk on the earth and take care of everything in it, just like God told them to. We have a job.

A scoundrel is a mean, worthless, uncaring person. We are talking about heroes. Adam and Eve weren't heroes; neither were they scoundrels, but you can't understand the rest of the Bible unless you know about Adam and Eve, so here is their story.

Adam and Eve

God planted a garden eastward in Eden. There He put the man that He had created. He named him Adam. God told Adam that he could eat of every tree in the garden, but he was not to eat of the Tree of the Knowledge of Good and Evil in the middle of the garden, because if he did, he would die.

God brought all the animals to Adam and told him to name them, so Adam named all the animals. We don't know how long Adam and God walked together, but we know that in the cool of the evening, God came down and visited Adam.

Adam noticed that each one of the animals had a mate. There was a male and a female of every kind, but there was no one for Adam.

God said, "It is not good for the man to be alone." He put Adam into a deep sleep, and took out one of his ribs. Around that rib, He formed a woman, and when He woke Adam up, He presented him with his helper, this beautiful woman.

Adam called her "woman" because she was taken out of man- -not out of his head to rule over him, or out of his feet so he could walk on her, but out of his side to be his companion and helper. He named her Eve.

Woman came from man, and ever after, man came from woman, so God had made a loving circle of humanity, each depending on the other.

Adam was so excited to have Eve. He adored her! With Eve there, it didn't seem so long from evening to evening when God came down to talk to them.

But one day as they were walking in the garden, a serpent came up to them and began to talk to Eve. He said, "Did God say that you can't eat everything in the garden?"

Eve answered, "We can eat of every tree in the garden, but not of the fruit of the tree in the middle of the garden. God said, "Don't even touch it, or you will die!" (Adam had probably added that part about not even touching it, to keep her away from it.)

The serpent answered, "Oh, you won't die. God knows that you will be like gods. You will know good and evil." (He tried to make God out to be a liar).

Eve was very naive and listened to the serpent. She touched the fruit, took a bite and saw that it tasted good. As she was eating it, she gave some to Adam, who was standing there with her, and he ate it, too.

Now, here was Adam's chance to be a hero, but he blew it. Adam knew what God had said. He wasn't tempted by the serpent, but he didn't want to make Eve mad at him, so he just let her do what she was tempted to do, and went along with it. He put Eve's wishes before God's commands, and fell into disobedience right along with her. If he had led her away or said something to her, perhaps she would not have led them both into sin, but he wimped out.

As soon as they had disobeyed, they looked at each other and realized that they were both naked. Their robes of righteousness had burned up with their disobedience. They scurried around and made themselves some slapped together clothes out of leaves.

That night, when God came down to talk with them, they hid. God knew what they had done and where they were, but He called to them, anyway: "Adam, where are you?"

Adam and Eve came out and God asked them why they were hiding. They answered that they were naked, so they hid.

God said, "Did you eat of the tree of which I told you not to eat?"

Adam said, "That woman, YOU gave me, gave me of the tree, and I ate."

Eve said, "The serpent tempted me, and I ate." Each was blaming someone else. "Not me! Not me!!"

God told the serpent, "Since you let Satan use you, you will have to crawl on the ground on your stomach all your life from now on. You and the woman and her children will be enemies. You will try to bite them. BUT ONE OF THEM WILL STEP ON YOU AND CRUSH YOU! He was speaking to Satan. This is the first promise from God that He had a way out for them, a way they could come back after their disobedience---a Savior.

To Eve, He said, "Childbirth will be more difficult for you. You were equal here, but now your husband will rule over you." (This was not a curse; it was just a result of bringing sin into the world.) To Adam, He said, "Because you listened to your wife instead of me, the ground is cursed to you. It will no longer give up its fruit easily. Thorns and thistles will grow. You will work hard to feed yourself and your family, all your life, until you die and your body returns to the dust of the ground from which you were taken." (Notice, they were not cursed, only the ground was cursed, but they had let sin into the world. Now they had to live with it.)

God made coats of skin and dressed them. Then He sent them out of the garden to fend for themselves, with work to do; because, if they stayed, they would eat of the other tree in the garden, the "Tree of Life," and live forever in their sins.

Again, Cain was wicked, and righteous Abel didn't live that long, but you need to know their story.

Cain and Abel

I think both Adam and Eve were a little hard to get along with for awhile after they were kicked out of the garden. Each of them blamed the other. There was probably a lot of quarreling, but they were all they had, so they had to get along the best they could.

I think that they had many girls, but when they finally had a baby boy, they were thrilled, and thought maybe this baby was the promise that God had given them of a savior to crush the serpent's head.

I think they spoiled Cain, dreadfully. He thought the world revolved around him, so when a little brother, Abel, was born, he wasn't happy. He really never got to love that little brother. He stayed jealous of him even when they were grown up.

Cain became a farmer, but Abel was a keeper of sheep. After awhile, each of them decided to bring an offering to God.

Abel loved God and was serving him. He brought the very best of his flock. He was willing to do everything God's way.

Cain couldn't care less. He slapped together some of the produce he had raised and gave it as an offering to God.

God accepted Abel's offering, but He didn't accept Cain's offering. This made Cain very angry with God, but he blamed Abel. He thought Abel had bested him again, and displaced him, even with God.

God told Cain, "If you do right, you will be accepted; but if you have the wrong attitude, sin is there in you. Be careful that it doesn't get the best of you!"

Cain was so angry with God and his brother. He made a plan to beat Abel up. He asked Abel to come with him into the field; and while they were there, Cain killed his brother, Abel. I don't think Cain knew he could actually kill Abel in his anger, but he did. He didn't think anyone knew it, because nobody saw him do it, but God did.

God came to Cain and asked him,"Where is your brother, Abel?"

Cain snarled back, "Am I my brother's keeper?"

God didn't let him get away with his evasion. God said, "What have you done? Your brother's blood calls to me from the ground, and now that ground, which you love, is cursed to you. Nothing will grow for you, anymore. You will be a fugitive and a wanderer in the earth from now on."

Cain thought his punishment was more than he could stand and everyone who saw him would try to kill him. So God set a mark upon Cain to protect him and let people know they were not to kill him.

Then Cain went out from the presence of the Lord and lived in the land of Nod, on the east side of Eden. Cain found a wife and they had a son, Enoch. Cain built a city and named it after his son.

He had other sons, and they had sons and daughters. They did all kinds of things: Some were musicians, some were ranchers; some worked with brass and iron. They were mighty men, but they didn't seem to have anything to do with God.

But God was not through with Adam and Eve. He gave them another son, along with their many daughters. This son they named Seth. Eve believed that God was giving them another son to take the place of Abel, whom Cain had killed. Seth loved God and raised his sons to know God and serve Him. Then people began to call on the name of the Lord, again.

After Seth was born, Adam and Eve had many, many children. When Adam was nine hundred thirty years old, he died, just as God had said that he would.

Seth lived nine hundred and twelve years. He had many children also. His son, Enos, served God all his nine hundred and five years. He had many children and he also died. Each one lived almost 1000 years, but they died, just as God had warned that they would if they disobeyed. God keeps his word!

Adam lived 930 years; Seth lived 912 years; Enos lived 905 years; Kenan lived 910 years; Mahalaleel lived 895 years; Jared lived 962 years.

Jared had a son named Enoch. Enoch lived on earth 365 years. He lived so close to God, that God just took him home to heaven. He didn't even have to die--God just took him. Enoch's son, Methuselah, became the oldest living person, ever. He lived to be 969 years old.

After that, God said that He was going to limit the ages of men. They would no longer live almost 1000 years. God decided that people had too much time to get into wickedness. From now on, God was going to begin to limit life to 120 years.

Methuselah had a son, Lamech, who had a son called Noah.

Noah was a hero because he believed God and did what God told him to do, even when it didn't make any sense to him. It had never rained, and he lived in an arid land; why would one build a boat in the middle of a desert?!

Noah

Noah had three sons, named, Shem, Ham and Japheth. They may have been triplets, but probably they are mentioned that way because all of them stayed close to God and helped Noah build the ark.

Up to this time, it had never rained. The earth was watered by a mist that came up from the ground.

Except for the mist, Noah lived in a dry land. People knew nothing about rain, but God told Noah to build an ark out in the middle of this dry country. He told him exactly how to build it, and why. God said that the whole earth was so full of violence and wickedness that He was going to destroy it. He wanted Noah to build this boat so that he and his family would be saved when the rains came.

Noah didn't understand what rain was, but he knew who God was. He served God, even though all the people around him did not. Noah's sons knew that if their father said that God talked to him and told him something, they believed him. They all stayed and helped him build the ark, just as God had instructed.

It took them about 100 years to get the ark built. All the time they were building, they were telling people about God and trying to get them interested in getting into the ark when the time was right, but nobody listened.

When the ark was finished, all the animals began to come, two by two, a male and a female of every kind--cattle, creeping things, birds. Of the clean animals, instead of just two, there were seven.

Noah got food for the animals. Noah had built rooms in the ark so everything had a place to stay and be safe from the flood that was coming.

God told Noah that it was time for his family--his wife, his three sons and their wives, to get into the ark.

When they were all in, with all the animals, it began to rain. And God shut the door. Nobody else could get in. Even if they suddenly decided they had been wrong, it was too late.

It rained for 40 days and 40 nights. All the deep places of the earth broke open and water covered the whole earth, even the mountain tops. Everything not in the ark, unless it lived in the water and could swim, drowned. The water stayed on the earth for 150 days.

God had not forgotten Noah. It finally quit raining. Then God made a wind to blow over the earth to dry up the water. The water gradually went down. Noah could see the tops of the mountains. He rejoiced!

God had had Noah put a window looking up, in the ark, so Noah opened the window and let a raven fly out. The raven went back and forth to the ark. Next, Noah sent out a dove. The dove could find no place to land, so she returned to Noah, who reached out and pulled her back in. Noah waited another week. Then he let the dove go, again. This time, she came back with an olive leaf in her beak! He waited seven more days and sent the dove out, again. This time she didn't return.

Finally, Noah took the covering off the ark and looked. The ground was dry. God told him it was time to leave the ark and let everything in it go free. (Some modern day pilots think that they have seen Noah's ark buried in the ice of Mt. Ararat. Wouldn't that be something to find?)

Noah built an altar and sacrificed a burnt offering of thanksgiving to the Lord for sparing them all.

God said that He would not destroy the entire earth with a flood again. He put a rainbow in the sky as a sign of his covenant to all that while the earth remains, planting and harvest, cold and heat, summer and winter, day and night, will always be.

God started over again with Noah and his sons to replenish the earth. He told Noah that all animals would be afraid of him, and he was in charge of them. He could eat meat, as well as fruits. Noah lived 950 years; then he died.

After the flood, God told people to scatter all over the earth, use it, and take care of it. People settled wherever they wanted to; but most of them wanted to live together. They wanted to make a name for themselves. They built a city and tried to build a tower to reach up to heaven so they could bring God down to their level.

It was called the "Tower of Babel" because God confused their language so that they could not understand one another. They couldn't work together, so they scattered as God had told them to do.

For a long time after that, nobody seemed to remember the Creator God. They began to worship the sun, the moon and the stars. When there was anything they could not understand, they made a god of it; and there was so much they couldn't understand!

The people of Ur of the Chaldees, were moon worshippers. There was a man there whose name was Abram. He seemed to be the only person on earth at the time who was listening to God.

Perhaps his father heard, too, but his hearing was not enough to keep him obeying the dream. He took his family as far as Haran and stopped there, where he died.

So, our next hero is Abram. God changed his name to Abraham. He followed God and did what God told him, even when it didn't make a lot of sense to him. He believed God, and God said, "That is the kind of person I want."

Abram

In Haran, The Lord had said to Abram, "Leave your country, and your father's house and all your relatives, and go to a land that I will show you. I will make a great nation out of your descendants. I will bless you and make you famous. You will be a blessing. I WILL USE YOU SO THAT ALL THE FAMILIES OF THE EARTH WILL BE BLESSED BECAUSE OF YOU."

So, Abram did as God had told him. He took all his possessions and his wife, Sarai, who was a half sister that he had married. His nephew, Lot, wanted to go with him, so he also took Lot and his family and all their servants and went into the land of Canaan. God told him that some day all the land would be his. He built an altar to God and worshiped him. But there was a famine in the land at that time, so Abram took all his possessions and people and went down to Egypt to stay until the famine was over.

Abram was awfully new at serving God. He knew that often men were killed so powerful men could take their wives, if they were beautiful.

Sarai was very beautiful. So, Abram told Sarai to tell everybody that she was Abram's sister, instead of telling them that she was also his wife. So, that is what Sarai did.

When they got to Egypt, sure enough, people saw Sarai and told the Pharaoh about her. He had a habit of collecting every beautiful woman he found and adding them to his harem. Pharaoh took Sarai into his house to marry her, too.

Pharaoh treated Abram very well, giving him cattle and oxen, donkeys and maidservants and menservants in exchange for Sarai, thinking she was Abram's sister. Lot, as a relative, got in on the blessing, too.

When Pharaoh found out that Sarai was Abram's wife, as well as his half-sister, he was very displeased with Abram. He gave Sarai back to him and kicked him out of the country, with all that he had.

Abram had become very rich. He went back to Canaan, where he had built the altar. Lot went with him.

They were both so rich and had so many sheep and cattle and livestock that there was not enough grass for both of their herds. Their herdsmen began to fight over grass.

Abram told Lot. "Let's not fight over it. You choose where you want to live and I will go the other direction".

Though Abram was the older and should have had all of it, he gave Lot his choice. Lot chose the best land, the well watered plain of Jordan, and started toward the city of Sodom.

After Lot left, God came again to Abram and told him that everything he could see, all the land, was to be his. God promised he would give it to Abram's children.

Abram had no children. His wife, Sarai, was barren, but Abram believed what God told him and waited for the children God was going to give him.

In the meantime, four powerful kings in the area went to war against five kings. One of the five kings was the king of Sodom. Now, Lot had settled in Sodom, with his family, and become a part of it.

The other kings won the battle, and took Lot and his family and all the other people of Sodom prisoners, along with all their cattle, food, and valuables.

Someone escaped and went to Abram and told him what had happened. Abram armed all his fighting men, 318, from his household, with all his friends who would help, and set out to rescue Lot. He attacked in the night and beat the enemy and rescued all the people and goods.

As they came back, Melchizedek, the God worshipping King of Salem, met them and blessed Abram and thanked God for delivering the enemy into Abram's hands. As a "Thank Offering" to God, Abram gave him a tenth of everything, a "tithe."

When, the king of Sodom came out to meet them, he told Abram, "Give me the people of Sodom. You take the goods for yourself."

Abram told him, "No, I won't take anything that is yours, not even a shoe string. I don't want you to ever be able to say that you made me rich! Just give the young men who went with me, Aner, Eshcol, and Mamre, their share."

After this, God came to Abram in a dream, telling him, "Don't be afraid, I am your shield, and your exceeding great reward."

Abram told God that he had no son to come after him. God promised him that he would have a son of his own and that his descendants would be as many as the stars in the sky. Abram believed what the Lord said. God said that because he believed, He was pleased with him.

God reminded Abram that it was God who had brought Abram out of Ur to Canaan to give him the land there. God said that He was going to make a covenant with Abram. A covenant was a binding agreement between two people, so strong, that if one of them broke the agreement, he was to die just like the animals did.

God told Abram to lay out the animals for a covenant: a heifer, a nanny goat, and a ram-all 3-year-olds, and a young pigeon, with a trench between the halves. This was the way they made a binding agreement at that time.

Abram divided each of the animals in half and laid each piece one against another. As he killed them, the blood ran down into the trench. The thing to do was for each of the partners to walk through the blood to confirm the covenant. This was to signify that if either one broke the covenant, his blood would be shed like these animals and he would die.

Abram waited for a sign from God. He waited and waited. Vultures came down to eat the sacrifice, but Abram chased them off. All day, he chased them away. Finally, when the sun went down, Abram fell into a deep sleep, with a horror of darkness coming to him.

God spoke to Abram in the darkness and told him that his descendants would be captives in a strange land for 400 years, but would afterward come out and return to Canaan, because it was not yet time for Abram to have Canaan.

Then, in the dark, a smoking furnace and a burning lamp passed between those pieces of sacrifice/covenant. It was God walking through the blood to confirm the covenant. Abram never did go through it; he knew he couldn't keep it.

God was showing him that all salvation is from God. God has to do it all. All man can do is accept it, say, "Thank You," and live for God.

When Sarai was in Egypt, Pharaoh had given her a maid servant to take care of her. They had brought that maid along with them when they came back to Canaan. Her name was Hagar.

Sarai had not been able to have children. She knew what God had promised Abram and she decided to help him out. She convinced Abram to take Hagar as a second wife so any children Hagar had, Sarai could claim as hers. That was the custom of that day.

Abram listened to Sarai, and married Hagar. But when Hagar became pregnant, she looked down on Sarai, and was snotty to her. Sarai was furious! She blamed Abram. Abram told her, "Do whatever you want with her. She is your servant."

Sarai was mean to Hagar, so mean that Hagar ran away into the wilderness. She was very angry. She found a fountain of water and sat there. God sent an angel to talk to her.

The angel said, "Hagar, Sarai's maid, what are you doing here? Go back to Sarai, and do what she tells you. God is giving you a son. You are to call his name Ishmael. He will be a loner, but God will make him a great man. And he will have many descendants."

Hagar was so impressed that Abram's God would talk to her, a woman and a foreigner, that she called the name of the place, Beer-lahai-roi (You are the God who sees me).

She went back and behaved until she gave birth to Ishmael, Abram's first son. Abram was 86 years old when Ishmael was born. Abram loved Ishmael and Sarai treated him as her son. He perhaps didn't even know that Hagar was really his mother.

When Abram was ninety-nine years old, God came to him again and promised him that he would be a father of many nations. God changed Abram's name to Abraham, and told him that He was establishing his covenant with him and his descendants. He would give Abraham a son and He would give his descendants the land of Canaan. He told him that every male child was to be circumcised, when he was eight days old, as a token between him and God.

God also told Abraham that his wife, Sarai's name was to be changed, too. She was to be called Sarah. Sarah would have a son, and she would be a mother of nations.

Abraham fell down laughing, thinking: I am almost 100 years old, and Sarah is nearly 90 years old. Will we have a child now? Then Abraham asked God to bless Ishmael and keep him faithful to God.

God replied, "Yes, I will bless Ishmael. I will make him great; but Sarah's child, who will be born next year, and named Isaac, is the one with whom I am making my covenant."

Abraham circumcised all the males in his household. Abraham was 99 years old, and Ishmael was 13 when Abraham did as God had commanded him.

One day, as Abraham was sitting in the door of his tent, he saw three men coming toward him. He invited them in for refreshments, sent Sarah to make cakes for them, and got a calf and had it butchered. This was the way one welcomed strangers in the desert.

After he'd fed them, one of them asked, 'Where is Sarah, your wife?"

Abraham replied, "In the tent." (God had already told Abraham; now He needed to tell Sarah the good news of her baby.)

The man told him. "I will come back in a year and Sarah will have a son."

Sarah was behind the door. When she heard him, she laughed in her heart. "I am far too old to have a baby now, and Abraham is old, too!"

The man knew that Sarah had laughed. When Sarah denied laughing, He said, "Yes you did! You WILL have a son. Is anything too hard for the Lord?"

Then the men got up and started in the direction of the city of Sodom. Abraham walked along with them for a ways, as was the custom of treating guests well.

As they walked along, God said, "I don't think I should hide what I am about to do, from Abraham."

He knew Abraham would intercede. So, He began to tell Abraham about how sinful Sodom and Gomorrah were. As they talked, the two angels kept going on toward Sodom.

When Abraham realized what God was planning to do, he began to bargain with him. He knew that Lot lived in Sodom, so Lot's life was about to be destroyed.

He asked God, "Will you destroy the good along with the wicked? What if there are 50 good men in Sodom. Will you still destroy it?"

God said, "If I find 50 good men in the city I will not destroy it."

Abraham said, "I am nothing, but since I've already begged for 50, what about 45?" God relented for 45.

Abraham kept going, down to ten, in his bargaining.

God said, "I will not destroy Sodom if ten righteous men can be found."

Then God went on His way and Abraham went back to his tent.

When the two angels got to Sodom, they found Lot sitting in the gate, the place where city business was done. Lot invited them to his house.

They said they would spend the night in the streets. Lot begged them to come home with him. He knew they would not be safe in the streets of Sodom. They came home with Lot. Lot gave them supper.

A wicked mob stormed Lot's house that night. The angels took Lot out of Sodom before they destroyed it. He was the only good man in that city. Though he was good, he had put himself in a wicked place and he lost most of his family in his foolishness.

He is not a hero, but God did not forget Lot, totally; one of his descendants, Ruth, became the grandmother of King David and the ancestor of Jesus, the Messiah.

Abraham left the place where he was and went south, into the territory of King Abimelech. He knew Abimelech's reputation for taking beautiful women, so he used the same tactics he had used with Pharaoh. You would think he would have learned his lesson, but maybe he had gotten so wealthy from that experience that he didn't think of it as bad as it was. At any rate, he told Sarah to say that she was his sister, and not mention that she was also his wife.

Sarah was still beautiful. Thinking she was Abraham's sister and he would honor Abraham by marrying his sister, Abimelech took Sarah into his house to be his wife. But God gave the king a terrible dream, telling him that if he didn't return Abraham's WIFE to him he would die, and everything he had would die, too. Abimelech was really upset with Abraham, but God had told him that Abraham was a prophet and he would pray for him, and they would all be able to have children again.

When Abimelech asked Abraham why he had done such a terrible thing, Abraham told him that it was only a half truth: Sarah was his half sister, as well as his wife. He had asked her to lie to protect him.

Abimelech gave rich gifts to Abraham and gave Sarah back to him. God had protected them again, even when they didn't trust Him like they should have.

Within the year, after God had visited them, Sarah had a son. She and Abraham were thrilled beyond measure! They named their son, Isaac, as God had told them to.

When he was eight days old, Abraham circumcised him. Abraham was 100 years old when Isaac was born and Sarah was 90.

Isaac's name means "Laughter." Sarah said, "Now everybody will laugh along with me. God has made me laugh."

When Isaac was old enough to be weaned, Abraham gave a great feast for him. As all were celebrating, Ishmael felt jealous of this little boy who seemed to take his place. He made fun of him. Sarah saw it and was furious.

She told Abraham."Get rid of this bond woman and her son. Ishmael will never be an heir with my son, Isaac."

Abraham loved Ishmael and it made him very sad. But God said, "Do what Sarah says, I will look after Ishmael, but my covenant is with Isaac."

So, early in the morning, Abraham gave Hagar bread and water to take with them and sent them away, probably to meet a camel train to go back to Egypt. He was giving her her freedom and her son, Ishmael. They set out, but they got lost in the desert of Beer-sheba. The food was gone. The water was all gone. It was hot and dry and they didn't know where they were or where the camel train was supposed to be. They both thought they would die. Fourteen-year-old Ishmael was crying, and Hagar sat down a long ways away from him, because she didn't want to see him die. Hagar cried bitterly.

God heard their cries and sent an angel to show Hagar the well of water nearby. So Hagar got water for both of them. They found the camel train and safety.

Ishmael grew to be a strong man, who became an archer and lived in the wilderness. His mother got an Egyptian wife for him.

A long time later God spoke to Abraham, and told him to take his son, Isaac, and go to the land of Moriah and offer him up to God for a burnt offering.

Isaac was a young man, probably stronger than his father, because he was the one who carried the wood.

It was customary in that time, for men to offer to their idol god, one of their sons. It was supposed to give them good luck and put them in favor with their god.

Abraham loved God supremely, so when God told him to sacrifice Isaac, he just set out to do it. Abraham knew God's voice so well.

Abraham loved his son so much! He knew that Isaac was the son God had promised him. God had said that He would bless the world through him. So, Abraham must have thought that God either would bring Isaac back from the dead or something; he didn't know what. He just knew to obey God. So he did.

Three days later, they got to the mountain that God pointed out to Abraham. Abraham took Isaac, his son, put the wood on his back, took the fire and the knife in his own hand, and set out for the mountain.

He told the two servants he had brought with them, "I and the lad will be back after we have worshipped."

As they walked along, Isaac questioned his Dad, "I have the wood, and you have the knife, but where is the lamb for the sacrifice?"

Abraham answered, "God will provide the sacrifice, my son."

When they got there, Abraham built an altar and put the wood on it. Then he tied his son's hands and laid him on the altar.

As he stretched out his hand to kill Isaac an angel of the Lord stopped him.

He called out, "Abraham! Abraham! Do not touch the lad. Don't lay a hand on him! Now I know that you love me better than anything or anyone." *(Of course, God always knew that, but I don't think Abraham did. He loved Isaac so very much!)*

When Abraham looked around, there behind him, caught in a bush, was a ram. Abraham took the ram and offered it in place of his son. Isaac was big enough to have kept Abraham from putting him on the altar, but he so trusted his father that he did whatever Abraham wanted him to do.

God blessed them both for being obedient. GOD GAVE THEM MORE PROMISES OF INHERITING THE LAND AND BEING A BLESSING TO THE WORLD.

God also told them that He never wanted them to sacrifice their children to Him or any other god from then on. Their children were precious to Him.

Abraham's wife, Sarah, was 127 years old when she died. Though God had promised the whole land to Abraham, Abraham didn't own even an acre of it. He had to beg for someone to sell him a place to bury Sarah.

One of the neighbors was kind to him and sold him the cave in the field of Machpelah before Mamre. So Sarah was buried in Canaan.

Isaac

Abraham was old. Isaac still didn't have a wife. Abraham sent his chief servant to go to his brother's country, and from his brother's household, find a wife for Isaac. He was not to marry him to a Canaanite woman or to take Isaac back to the land from which they had come.

Fathers had all the say in those times. Children did not grow up as fast as they do these days. They were still called "a lad" when they were 40 years old.

Abraham promised the servant that God would go with him and prosper his journey and show him the right wife for Isaac. The servant swore an oath to Abraham, and set out for Mesopotamia, where Abraham's brother, Nahor, lived, taking ten camels loaded down with rich gifts.

He got to the city, and stopped at a well of water, just at the time the girls from the city were coming out to draw water for their flocks of sheep.

The servant prayed, "Lord God of my master Abraham, I beg you, be kind to my master, Abraham, and let it be that the girl whom I ask for a drink, will give me a drink, and tell me that she will water my camels, too. Let that be the girl whom you have chosen for my master, Isaac."

While he was still praying, Rebekah, Abraham's brother's granddaughter, came out and did exactly as the servant had asked God to provide.

He watched her as she got all the water and carried it to his camels. Then he asked her," Whose daughter are you?"

When he heard who she was, the servant thanked the Lord for guiding him and went to her house with her.

He told her family exactly what had happened, how God had guided him, who he was, all about their relative, Abraham, and how rich he was.

He asked for them to let Rebekah come back to his country with him to marry Isaac.

After he gave all of them rich gifts, he persuaded them to let Rebekah go with him right away. Her brother wanted the servant to stay longer, but he wanted to go home as soon as possible.

So Rebekah went with the servant to go be Isaac's wife, taking with her all her servant girls.

Isaac was out in the field meditating in the evening when he looked up and saw a camel caravan coming. He went out to meet it.

When she saw him, Rebekah asked, "Who is that man?"

The servant answered: "That is my master's son, Isaac, the man who is to be your husband."

So Rebekah put on her veil and waited for Isaac to come to her. Isaac took Rebekah for his wife. He loved her and she was a comfort to him after losing his mother.

Abraham was lonely after Isaac married. He had never wanted another wife as long as Sarah was alive, but now he found another wife, named Keturah.

He and Keturah had six sons. When they got old enough, Abraham gave each of his sons gifts and sent them away to the east country, away from Isaac.

Abraham lived to be 175 years old. When he died, his sons, Isaac and Ishmael, buried him in the cave at Machpelah, where Sarah was buried. He still had not seen the promise of God to own the land, but he died trusting. He knew that God is faithful.

Isaac was 40 years old when he married Rebekah but they had no children for 20 years.

Finally, Isaac prayed and asked God for a son. God granted his request and Rebekah became pregnant.

She was so uncomfortable, she asked God why. He told her that she was carrying twins and the one born second would be greater than the firstborn.

The one who was born first was named Esau. When the second one came out, he was holding onto Esau's foot. They named him Jacob (meaning, he cheats).

Esau became a good hunter. His father favored him.

Jacob stayed around home. He was his mother's favorite.

The parents played favorites and the boys suffered for it. Jacob was a mama's boy and sort of sneaky. Esau was Daddy's hunter and proud of it.

One day when Esau came home from hunting, he was very hungry. Jacob was making some stew and it smelled good. Esau asked Jacob to give him some stew because he said he was starving!

Instead of giving it to him like a good brother should, Jacob bargained with his brother. He asked for his birthright---the rights of being born first. Jacob had always wanted it, but it didn't mean a thing to Esau, so he sold it to Jacob for a bowl of stew and some bread. Then he got up and went away. He didn't realize what he had done until much later, but by then it was too late.

There was another famine in the land. God told Isaac not to go to Egypt, but to go where He told him, so Isaac went to King Abimelech's country like his father, Abraham, had. God promised that he would take care of Isaac and bless him. He gave him the same promises He had given Abraham about the land and many descendants, but Isaac was afraid.

He followed Abraham's lack of faith and told everyone that Rebekah was his sister instead of his wife. Because she was so beautiful he feared for his own life. With Abraham, it was a half truth. Of course, with Isaac, it was a total lie.

King Abimelech wasn't so easily taken in a second time. He asked Isaac why he had told a lie, and Isaac told him. Abimelech scolded Isaac, but let him live in the land.

The Lord blessed Isaac greatly, until he became so rich that the Philistines were afraid of him and began to fill in the wells of water Isaac had dug.

Finally, they made an agreement with each other, and they let his wells alone so Isaac could live in peace.

Isaac's son, Esau, married two women, two Hittite girls. His parents were not happy about it. Jacob was still at home. He was not married.

Isaac was old and almost blind. He didn't think he would live too much longer, so he called Esau to him one day. He told him "Go out and hunt. Then fix the wild game meat that I like so well. Bring it to me and I will give you your blessing."

Rebekah heard all this and she called her favorite, Jacob, and sent him out to kill two goats so she could make Isaac the food Isaac liked and have Jacob get Esau's blessing. She had it all planned out, and Jacob followed her instructions.

Since Esau was a hairy man, she put goat skins on Jacob to deceive Isaac. Then Jacob went in to his father, pretending to be Esau.

Isaac said, "The voice is Jacob. Come near so I can feel you.",

Rebekah had put some of Esau's clothes on Jacob so he would feel and smell like his brother, and he did.

He fooled his father and Isaac gave him the blessing he had intended to give Esau, but not the one he had planned to give Jacob.

Jacob had hardly gotten out when Esau came in and said; "Father, here is the food I have fixed for you. Now give me my blessing."

Isaac was horrified when he realized that he had been tricked.

Esau wept and pleaded, "Father, don't you have a blessing for me, too?"

Isaac said, "I have given your brother the fat of the land and said his brothers are to serve him. All I can say is that later you will shake off Jacob's yoke."

Esau hated his brother for stealing his blessing and cheating him out of his birthright. He vowed that as soon as their father died, he would kill Jacob.

Rebekah was so concerned that she told Jacob and sent him off to her brother, Laban, to stay until Esau got over his anger and the desire to kill him. She told Isaac that it was because she so hated the wives Esau had married and she wanted Jacob to get a wife from her brother's family.

Isaac called Jacob in and gave him his rightful blessing, the blessing of Abraham, and sent him off to find a wife from his mother's relatives.

When Esau realized how distasteful his wives were to his parents, he went and found a granddaughter of Ishmael for a third wife.

Jacob did not act like a hero for the first few years of his life, but after he met God, was cheated by his uncle, and wrestled with God, he was a changed man and God was able to use him. He became a Bible Hero in spite of himself. God used him to establish the Hebrew nation. His twelve sons and their descendants became the Nation of Israel.

Jacob

Jacob set out all alone to go to a strange land where he knew nobody, even if they were related. He walked all day. That night, he piled up some stones for a pillow and lay down, probably thinking about how badly he had managed his life so far.

As he slept, he dreamed. He saw a ladder set up on the earth with its top reaching to heaven; and all night the angels of God went up and down it. The Lord stood at the top and talked to him. God said, "I am the God of your father, Isaac, the God of your grandfather, Abraham, and I will be your God, too. I will give you all the land that I promised to your fathers. I will be with you in this strange land where you are going. I will prosper you and bring you safely back to this place."

Jacob woke in the morning and realized that God had spoken to him. He said. "The Lord is in this place and I didn't know it! God, if you will do all you said, I will serve you, always."

Jacob built an altar of the stones and worshipped God there. He called the place Bethel, which means "house of God." He continued in the strength of God's promise and presence.

The first person of the family to meet Jacob was Rachel, the daughter of his mother's brother, Laban. She was out tending the sheep when Jacob got to Haran. Jacob moved the stone protecting the well, so she could water her father's flocks. When she heard who he was, she took him home with her.

Laban had two daughters, Leah, the older one, and Rachel, who was very beautiful. Jacob stayed, and fell in love with Rachel. For pay, he bargained with Laban to work for him for seven years so he could marry Rachel. Finally, at the end of seven years, Jacob asked for his wife.

Laban made a great wedding feast for them and invited all the men of the place. In the dark, Laban exchanged Leah for Rachel , but Jacob didn't know until morning. When he found out he had been tricked, he was furious.

When he called Laban on it, Laban excused himself by saying that in their country it was a custom not to give the younger daughter in marriage until the older one was married. He said, "Give Leah her week of marriage; then you can have Rachel too, if you will work for me for another seven years."

At that time it was customary for a man to have as many wives as he could take care of. With the daughters, Laban gave each of them their serving girls, Zilpah for Leah, and Bilhah for Rachel.

Jacob loved Rachel, but he just put up with Leah. God was merciful to Leah, and gave her four sons: Reuben, Simeon, Levi, and Judah.

Rachel couldn't seem to have children. She was jealous of her sister, so she gave Jacob her maidservant, Bilhah, for a wife so she could claim Bilhah's children as her own. Bilhah had two sons, Dan and Naphtali.

Leah was not to be outdone, so she gave Jacob her maidservant, Zilpah, for a wife. Zilpah had two sons, Gad and Asher.

Then Leah had another two sons, Issachar, and Zebulun, followed by a daughter, Dinah.

Finally, Rachel had a son of her own. They called him Joseph. After Joseph was born, Jacob went to Laban and told him that he needed to go back to his own country.

Laban convinced him to stay and work for him because he said that God had prospered him while Jacob was there.

Jacob agreed to stay and work. The agreement was for Jacob to go through all the flocks and take out all the speckled and spotted cattle, sheep, and goats for his wages. Laban agreed.

But then, Laban had his sons remove all the spotted, speckled, and brown ones and take them far into the hills so Jacob wouldn't get them. Jacob knew Laban did this, so he took poplar, almond, and plane trees, stripped the branches back so the stripes showed and put them where the animals bred. When the calves and lambs were born, they were striped. He put them in a separate place for himself. Jacob did all he could to get the strongest beasts to produce striped calves and lambs.

Jacob got very rich taking care of Laban's livestock. He also learned what it was like to be cheated and treated like he had treated his brother.

He worked for Laban 20 years, altogether. Finally, when Jacob heard Laban's sons complaining of how Jacob was getting rich off their father and Laban didn't seem to like him much anymore, he decided it was really time to go home. God told him to go and He would be with him.

Jacob took his wives out into the field and talked to them. He reminded them that their father had tricked him, and changed his wages ten times, but God had continued to prosper him.

They said, "Our father has sold us to you. We have nothing to gain staying here. If you think it is best, we are willing to leave."

Laban was out shearing sheep when Jacob loaded up his household and set out for Canaan without telling Laban he was leaving.

Before they left, Rachel stole the household images that were her father's and brought them along.

It was three days later when Laban finally found out that Jacob had left. He was very angry. He brought a lot of men and chased after Jacob for seven days. But the night before he caught up with Jacob, God gave him a dream. God said, "Be careful; don't speak to Jacob either good or bad."

So when Laban caught up with Jacob he simply asked." Why did you sneak away without letting me have a feast for my family before you left, so I could tell my children goodbye; and why did you steal my gods?" (the images were probably land titles).

Jacob didn't know about the idols Rachel had taken, so he told Laban to search out the camp. They searched, but Rachel sat on them, so they were never found and Laban went home.

It had been 20 years, but Jacob slowly started toward home. He had a huge amount of livestock, herdsmen, servants, both men and women, four wives and eleven sons and a daughter. God had blessed him mightily, just as He had promised.

Jacob still had some work to do, getting things right with the brother he had wronged. He sent servants to tell Esau that he was coming and how God had blessed him. He told them to call him "your servant, Jacob" when they spoke of him to Esau.

The servants came back and told Jacob, "Esau is coming to meet you, and he has four hundred men on horseback with him."

That scared Jacob half to death! He was convinced that Esau still had not forgiven him for his terrible deceit and was coming to kill him. Jacob divided all his goods and people into two groups, thinking at least one group should be able to escape.

He arranged a gift for Esau to perhaps lessen his anger. He picked out 200 nanny goats, 20 rams, 30 milk camels and their colts, 40 cows and ten bulls, 20 burros and their foals. He put them into the hands of his servants with the direction, "Go first, before all the people. Leave a space between each group. When my brother asks who all these belong to, tell him, 'They are a present to my Lord, Esau, from his servant, Jacob, and Jacob is coming behind us'."

That night, Jacob put all his family over on the other side of the brook. Then, he went back alone.

All night, he wrestled with a man. At daybreak, the man told Jacob, "Let me go."

Jacob said, "I will not let you go until you bless me."

The man touched Jacob's thigh and put it out of joint. Jacob still would not let go.

Then the man asked Jacob, "What is your name?"

Jacob had always been such a deceiver and had lived up to his name. He was still trying to get by, using his wits, but he was afraid it wasn't going to work, this time. Jacob said, "My name is Jacob."

The man told him, "Your name will no longer be Jacob. Your name is Israel, because you have wrestled with God and won." Jacob called the name of that place, Peniel, for he said he had seen God, face to face, and lived.

When Esau came with his 400 men, Jacob bowed down to him seven times as he came toward him.

Esau ran to meet him. He hugged him and kissed him and they both cried together. Then Esau wanted to meet all of Jacob's family. They all bowed down to Esau and showed him proper respect.

Esau asked, "What is all that drove of livestock I saw coming toward me for miles?"

Jacob was so grateful for God's protection. He told Esau "It is a gift to you, so you will forgive me."

Esau said, "I've got plenty already, keep your stuff."

But Jacob insisted, "If you really forgive me, please take the gift I have prepared for you as a sign that you no longer hate me."

So Esau finally agreed and took it. Esau wanted to escort Jacob home but Jacob was afraid to hurry all his animals and young family; so Esau went back home and Jacob and his family came along slowly by themselves.

They came to a place called Shalem, a city of Shechem in Canaan land. They built an altar, where Jacob worshipped the Lord.

Dinah, Jacob's daughter, went to see the girls in the city. Dinah was a beautiful girl. She had had no experience with getting along with strangers. She ran into trouble. Her experience showed her mother, Leah, that though Leah had always been jealous of her beautiful sister, Rachel, beauty could be a curse. It was to Dinah and her whole family.

They journeyed on to Ephrath, and Rachel gave birth to a second son. Her nurse had died, and she didn't have the help she needed. She died as her baby was born. His father named him Benjamin.

Jacob finally got home to his father, but his mother, Rebekah, had died, without ever seeing her son again. She paid a heavy price for her deception.

Isaac lived to be 180 years old. He died, and his sons, Jacob and Esau, buried him.

Esau and Jacob were both too rich in livestock to live together, so Esau went to Mt. Seir. Esau's family is called Edom. He had a large family, with many mighty men.

Joseph is our next hero. He is a real hero. As a lad, he made a few mistakes, but he overcame the hatred of his brothers, and loved them so much that he took care of them and their families, rather than get revenge. God blessed Joseph and helped him, especially in keeping the right attitude. Joseph shows us how to handle meanness and anger the right way.

Joseph

Jacob lived in Canaan. Now, Jacob had twelve sons. The older ones were grown men. Joseph was 17 years old; his little brother Benjamin was still young.

Jacob played favorites, too. Jacob loved Joseph more than his other children, because Joseph was Rachel's son, and was born in Jacob's old age. He made Joseph a special coat of many colors. That proved to the brothers that he was Jacob's favorite. They were mean to Joseph because of it.

One night, Joseph dreamed a strange dream; which he, unwisely, told to his brothers. They hated him for it. In the dream, they were all out in the field, binding grain sheaves. Joseph's sheaf stood upright, and all the other sheaves bowed down to it. He dreamed a second dream, where the sun, moon and eleven stars bowed down to his star. When he told his brothers and his father, Jacob scolded him for telling such a thing, but Jacob kept thinking about it. His brothers envied Joseph and hated him. They called him, "that dreamer."

His brothers went to feed their flocks in Shechem. They were gone a long time. After awhile, Jacob sent Joseph to see how they were. Joseph went to find his brothers. When he got there, he found that they had gone on to Dothan, so he followed them there.

While he was a long ways off, the brothers could tell it was Joseph coming toward them, because of his colorful coat. They plotted to kill him, so they would be rid of "that dreamer." The plan was to kill him, drop him into a pit and claim some wild animal had gotten him.

The oldest brother, Reuben, told them not to kill him, but instead, to put him into a pit nearby, and that would get rid of him.

Reuben was the one tending the sheep at the time. He planned to rescue Joseph later, but he didn't have the courage to face his brothers and make them behave. (Reuben was a wimp!)

When Joseph got there, they took off his coat of many colors and dropped him into an empty pit. Then they sat down to eat, leaving poor Joseph in the pit, hungry, wondering why they hated him so much and what would become of him.

While they were eating, a caravan of Ishmaelites came along, on their way to Egypt. One of the brothers, Judah, said, "Let's not kill Joseph; after all, he is our brother. Let's sell him to these Ishmaelites."

That sounded good to all the rest of them, so that is what they did. They sold him for twenty pieces of silver. Then they took his beautiful coat, dipped it in animal blood, took it to their father, and let him draw his own conclusions about Joseph being dead.

Reuben had come back to let Joseph out of the pit. He was horrified not to find him, but he went along with the rest of them in telling the lie to their father. None of them were prepared for the agony their father had over the death of his son. They all had to watch their father's grief for many years.

> *Righteous Abraham would have been appalled to see where his little pet lie had led: he told a half truth; Isaac told a full lie; Jacob stole from his brother and lied to his father; Jacob's sons sold their brother, and lied to their father. Family sins multiply!*

The Ishmaelites sold Joseph to Potiphar, an officer of Pharaoh and captain of the guard. Potiphar really liked Joseph. He saw how wise and well mannered he was and that God was with him. Potiphar put him in charge of all his house and everything he had. God blessed Potiphar greatly while Joseph was in charge.

Joseph was a handsome man and a godly one. Potiphar's wife liked what she saw. She tried to talk Joseph into going to bed with her. He refused over and over again. But one day all the men were somewhere else and nobody was in the house but the two of them. She grabbed hold of Joseph's coat to try to force him. He twisted out of his coat and ran out of the house, leaving his coat behind.

That was all that wicked woman needed. She hated to be made a fool, so she yelled, and told all the people who came that Joseph had tried to rape her, but she had screamed, and he had run off, leaving his coat behind.

When her husband came home she told him the same story.

Potiphar must have wondered about it, because he only had Joseph put in prison, instead of having him killed, as a slave would have been in those times.

God was still with Joseph in the prison, though. The keeper was kind to him and Joseph repaid the keeper by doing everything he could to help him. Soon, the keeper put Joseph in change of the prison. He trusted Joseph to take care of things, and he did

After awhile, two important officers of Pharaoh, the chief baker and the chief butler, landed in the prison where Joseph was. They had both offended Pharaoh. They stayed in prison for awhile. Joseph got to know them quite well.

One night, each of them had a dream. The dreams bothered them. They had no idea what they meant. Both of them looked sad. Joseph asked them what was the matter. They told him about having dreams.

Joseph told them, "Interpretations belong to God. Tell me what your dreams were; maybe God will tell me what they mean."

So the chief butler told his dream. He said, "I saw a vine with three branches with buds on it in front of me. As I watched, the buds burst into blossoms, then into clusters of ripe grapes. Pharaoh's cup was in my hand and I handed the cup to Pharaoh. He took it and drank from it."

Joseph interpreted the dream. He said," The three branches are three days. In three days, Pharaoh will restore you to your former position as butler. When he does, please remember me and tell him about me. I have done nothing wrong to deserve being here in this place."

The interpretation Joseph gave the butler encouraged the baker to tell his dream.

He said, "I dreamed I had three white baskets on my head. In the top basket were all kinds of baked goods for Pharaoh, but the birds came and ate them."

Joseph told him that his dream meant that in three days, Pharaoh would hang him and the birds would eat his flesh. Both dreams came true.

But, when he got out, the chief butler forgot all about Joseph. For two whole years more, Joseph stayed in jail, until one night, Pharaoh dreamed a strange dream. He sent for all his magicians and wise men and asked them to interpret his dream, but nobody could.

It was then that the chief butler finally remembered Joseph and told Pharaoh about him, how he had interpreted his and the baker's dreams and they both had come true.

Pharaoh sent for Joseph in the prison to come to him. So, Joseph shaved, cleaned himself up, dressed properly, and went to Pharaoh.

Pharaoh told him his dream. Pharaoh said, "I was standing by the river and up out of the river came seven fat cows, and they ate in the meadow. Then, after them came seven skinny, bad looking cows out of the river, and the skinny cattle ate up the fat ones. And I woke up. I fell asleep again and dreamed a second dream. In it, seven beautiful heads of grain came up on one stalk. Then seven bad, thin, heads of grain came up, and the bad ones ate up the good ones. Then I awoke. None of my wise men can tell me the meaning of the dream, but the butler says that you can."

Joseph told him, "Both dreams mean the same thing. God is showing Pharaoh what He is about to do. He told it twice because that means it is set and will happen soon. The seven good cows and the seven good heads of grain are both seven years of great plenty. The seven skinny cows and the seven skinny heads of grain are seven years so bad there will be a terrible famine in all the land."

Then Joseph told him, "Now let Pharaoh find a man wise enough to take care of it, and appoint officers to help him and gather up one fifth of everything that grows in the seven years of plenty. Put it into store houses, so that when the famine comes, people will have food to eat."

Pharaoh was so impressed, that he set Joseph, who knew what God was going to do, over all the land of Egypt, to do what Joseph had said needed to be done.

He dressed Joseph in finery, put a gold chain around his neck, and made him second only to Pharaoh in all the land of Egypt. He gave him an Egyptian name, and an Egyptian wife.

Joseph was 30 years old. He had spent 13 miserable years getting to know Egypt from the prison up. But now, God had honored him and Pharaoh honored him, and all of Egypt honored him.

Joseph and his wife had two sons, Manasseh and Ephraim.

For seven years, Joseph gathered up the extra food and put it in store houses. They had so much they could no longer count it. Storehouses were everywhere.Then the seven years of plenty were over and the famine began, when nothing would grow in all Egypt or anywhere else. The famine was great, just as Joseph had said it would be.

Reconciliation

The famine stretched into all the lands around Egypt. Everyone was in need of food. The people came to Joseph to buy food because there was no food anywhere except in the land of Egypt, in Joseph's storehouses.

When Jacob heard that there was grain to buy in Egypt, he sent his ten sons to Egypt to buy enough so the family could survive. He did not send Benjamin with them. He really didn't trust these ten sons of his. He remembered how Joseph had gone to them and disappeared. Benjamin was the only son he had left from Rachel. Though Benjamin was grown and had 10 sons of his own, he was still his father's "lad."

When the sons of Jacob got to Egypt to buy grain, they had to buy it from Joseph. They came and bowed down to him, just as in Joseph's dream. They didn't recognize Joseph, but he knew who they were.

Joseph remembered the dreams he'd had as a youth, how angry they had made his brothers, and how badly they had treated him. He didn't know whether he could trust them yet or not, so he spoke roughly to them and pretended that he thought they were spies. To persuade him that they were not spies, they told him about their father and brother at home, and that one brother was dead. Joseph told them to bring the youngest brother back with them to prove that what they said was true.

The brothers, not realizing Joseph understood what they said in Hebrew (he spoke to them through an interpreter), told each other that the trouble they were having was because they had been so mean to Joseph when he begged for his life. They all had guilty consciences.

Joseph went out and cried, then came back and tied up Simeon to keep in prison until they all returned with Benjamin.

Joseph commanded his servant to put each man's money back in his sack of grain. On the way home, when they opened the sacks to feed their animals, they found the money. Then they were really worried that God was punishing them for their treatment of Joseph!

When they got home and told their father about their trip, Jacob was worried about the man, too.

The famine continued and they ran out of food. The men refused to go back for more unless Benjamin went with them. They needed to get Simeon out of jail and they needed food, so finally Jacob let Benjamin go.

He didn't trust Reuben to care for Benjamin, but when Judah said that he would be responsible, he would bring him home safely, Jacob let him go. Jacob had them take presents to Joseph: honey, spices, almonds etc., double money, and Benjamin.

When Joseph saw Benjamin, he had the men all brought to his house for dinner. This really scared the brothers. Then, when they sat down to dinner, they found that they were seated from the oldest down to the youngest. How in the world did this man know their ages!

When Joseph saw his little brother, Benjamin, he just had to go out and cry before he could come back to dinner.

As an Egyptian, Joseph sat at a separate table, but visited with the brothers from there.

When they left, Joseph had his steward put all their money back in their sacks, and his own cup in the sack of Benjamin, the youngest. As soon as they were out of sight, Joseph sent his steward after them. When he caught up with them, he told them they had stolen Joseph's silver cup. The men knew they had not taken the cup, so they foolishly said, "Let the one in whose sack the cup is found die for it and the rest of us will be the man's servants."

The steward found the cup in Benjamin's sack, where he had put it. The brothers all tore their clothes in anguish and returned to Joseph's house.

Joseph told them all to go home. Benjamin would not die, but he was to stay and be his servant.

Judah pleaded with Joseph, telling him all about what had happened as far as Benjamin was concerned, and how if he didn't come home, their father would die of a broken heart, after having lost his other son, Benjamin's brother. Judah pleaded, "Let me stay and be your servant instead of my little brother, Benjamin. I promised my father that I would take care of him and if anything happens to him, my father will die of grief. Please let me stay in his place!"

When Joseph realized how much the brothers had changed, he couldn't stand it any longer. He sent all his servants out of the room, and told his brothers. "I am Joseph, your brother, whom you sold into Egypt. Don't be angry with yourselves any longer; for God sent me ahead of you to save your lives."

The brothers were shocked speechless! Joseph kissed all his brothers and cried over them. Of course, the servants heard all that was happening and reported to Pharaoh that Joseph's brothers had come.

Pharaoh told Joseph, "Tell your whole family to come down to Egypt and stay. There are five more years of famine. Since they are herdsmen, they can live in the area of Goshen."

Joseph sent a great caravan of food and carts to get his father and bring him and all their family and all their possessions to Egypt.

Jacob could hardly believe it when his sons told him that the man they had been so afraid of was Joseph, and Joseph was in command of all Egypt.

When he saw what Joseph had sent and heard his words, Jacob realized that Joseph was indeed alive, and that he could go and see him before he died.

Jacob had learned a few things about serving God, so he built an altar to God, and asked God if he should really go to Egypt as Joseph had asked them to. God told him, "Yes, Israel, go to Egypt and I will make of you a great nation there."

So Jacob (Israel) and all his family and all their belongings went to Egypt. In all, there were 66 people with him who went to Egypt. Counting Joseph and his family who were already there, Jacob's family numbered 70 people.

They were directed to the land of Goshen to live because they were shepherds.

Joseph went to Goshen to meet them. He hugged his father a long time as they cried on each other's shoulders. Jacob said that now he could die in peace because he had seen Joseph and knew that he was alive, after all.

Joseph arranged an audience with Pharaoh for his father. He took along five of his brothers and presented them to Pharaoh. Pharaoh told them, "Live in Goshen, and if there are good shepherds among you, take care of my livestock, too."

When Joseph brought his father in to Pharaoh, Pharaoh asked how old he was. Jacob told him, "I am 130 years old." Then Jacob blessed Pharaoh.

Joseph continued to sell food to all who came to him, but when the money ran out, people still kept coming, so Joseph bought their cattle and donkeys. The next year, Joseph bought the land for Pharaoh. Then he gave the people seed to plant. They were to give Pharaoh one-fifth of the crop when crops grew again.

Jacob and his sons lived in Goshen. They had many children.

Jacob lived another 17 years. When Jacob realized that he was dying, he called Joseph and had him promise that he would see that he was buried in Canaan, not in Egypt. Joseph promised.

Later, when Jacob got sick, Joseph heard of it, and took his two sons, Manasseh and Ephraim to him to be blessed. Jacob told him that those two boys should be named along with his sons. Jacob blessed the younger one above the older, saying that he would be greater, but both would be great and would be called 'Sons of Jacob'.

Then Jacob called all of his sons together to bless them before he died. He gave each of them the blessing they had coming to them. He passed over Reuben, as unstable, Simeon and Levi for their cruelty, and gave the blessing of Abraham to Judah. His would be the family the Messiah would come from: "THE LION OF THE TRIBE OF JUDAH." Jacob gave a special blessing to Joseph, because he had gone through so much. Then Jacob died. Joseph had his father embalmed, and the Egyptians mourned for him for 70 days, as their custom was. Then Joseph got permission from Pharaoh to go to Canaan to bury his father. All the important people of Egypt and all the family went up to Canaan to the cave of Machpelah and buried Jacob. It was a very great company.

After their father's death, the brothers went to Joseph and begged him to forgive them for the evil they had done to him. Joseph thought they already realized that he had forgiven them. It made him cry. He told them again, "Forgive yourselves. Though you meant evil, God brought good out of it. I will take care of all of you and your families."

Joseph lived to be 110 years old. He saw his grandchildren's children.

When he knew he was dying, Joseph told his relatives," God will take you out of Egypt someday (he remembered Abraham's vision) and take you back to Canaan. Promise me that when you go back, you will take my body with you. I want to be buried at home, in Canaan." They promised. Joseph died. He was embalmed and put in a coffin, in Egypt.

Our next hero is a man named Moses. He so trusted the Lord, that God gave him the courage and wisdom to lead all of his people out of slavery in Egypt and take them back to the Promised Land. It was an impossible task, but Moses stuck it out with God, and they actually got the job done, even though it took over forty years. Moses saw God's goodness and power. It was to Moses that God gave the Ten Commandments and showed him how people were to worship God. Moses is a real hero!

Baby Moses

Rebekah Jamison

Moses

Israel's family had lived in Egypt about four hundred years. They had become a great many people! In fact, there were so many that the new king over Egypt was afraid of them because there were more of them than there were Egyptians.

This pharaoh had never known Joseph, and he was worried that if the country went to war, the Israelites would fight with their enemies and overthrow them, so he made them slaves.

They built at least two treasure cities for Pharaoh: Pithom and Raamses.The Israelites had to do all the hard work, but they kept increasing. More babies were born all the time. Pharaoh called the midwives in and told them that if the baby was a daughter they could let it live, but if it was a son, they were to kill it.

The midwives, Shiphrah and Puah, would not do this terrible thing that the king had commanded, for they feared God. So, Pharaoh called them in and asked why they had not obeyed him. They told him that the Hebrew women had their babies before the midwives got there.

God blessed the midwives for serving him. The people of Israel multiplied and became very great in number. Pharaoh made a law that every daughter could be kept alive, but every son who was born was to be thrown into the Nile River.

There was a man and wife of the family of Levi. They had a son and a daughter; then they had a son at the time Pharaoh said to toss all boy babies into the Nile. They were not willing to kill their baby, so his mother hid him for three months.

When he got so big that his cries would be heard and they could no longer hide him, she built a little boat of papyrus with a cover, filled the cracks with tar and pitch, lined it with a blanket, and put the baby in it. She took it down to the river, and told her daughter to watch over it and see what happened. She knew that the princess bathed at that spot every day.

As the princess walked along the shore with her serving girls, she saw the little ark out among the rushes. She was curious and had her girl go get it.

When she opened the lid, the sun shone in the baby's eyes and he began to cry. She knew he was one of the Hebrew babies her father had said were to be killed. She felt sorry for him.

About that time, Miriam, the baby's sister, came up and asked the princess, "Shall I go and get a nurse from the Hebrew women so she can nurse the child for you?"

The princess said, "Go".

So, Miriam went and called her mother. The baby's mother came and took him home to care for him. When he got old enough, she took him to Pharaoh's daughter to be her son.

The princes named him Moses, because she said, "I drew him out of the water."

As Moses grew, he learned all the wisdom of Egypt. As the son of Pharaoh's daughter, he was taught, and treated, with great respect.

When Moses was grown, one day he went out to help oversee the slaves. While he was there, he saw an Egyptian beating a Hebrew, one of his people. He thought he would do what he could to help them, so he killed the Egyptian.

He thought nobody saw him. But the next day when he went out, he saw two Hebrews fighting. He tried to stop them, but the guilty one said, "Do you plan to kill me like you did the Egyptian yesterday?"

Moses knew that it was known what he had done and Pharaoh would get word of it. His life was in danger, so he ran away.

Pharaoh did try to find him to kill him; but he couldn't find him because Moses had gone out into the desert.

Moses went into the land of Midian and sat down by a well. The priest of Midian had seven daughters. They came to water their sheep. The men shepherds chased them away, but Moses helped the girls.

When they told their father why they were home so early, he said, "Where is the man? Go get him and bring him home to supper."

Moses stayed with the man, whose name was Jethro. Jethro gave Moses one of his daughters, Zipporah, for a wife. Moses stayed and looked after his father-in-law's sheep.

He and Zipporah had a son. They named him Gershom, for Moses said, "I have been a stranger in a strange land."

The king of Egypt died, and the new king worked the Hebrews even harder than his father. The people cried to God about their terrible time. God heard them.

God had promised Abraham that his people would be in Egypt 400 years, before they would get the Promised Land of Canaan. It was now almost 400 years. God had been preparing a man, though Moses didn't know it.

One day, as Moses was out in the desert tending Jethro's sheep, he saw in the distance, a bush on fire. As he watched, it burned and burned, but it didn't burn up. He went over to look at the bush to see what was going on. Out of the bush came a voice saying, "Moses, Moses, don't come any closer. Take off your shoes, for the ground you are standing on is Holy Ground. I am the God of your fathers, the God of Abraham, and Isaac, and Jacob." Moses hid his face. He was afraid to look at God.

God said, "I have seen the bad time my people, Israel, are having. I know how they are hurting. I am going to bring them out of Egypt and into Canaan, a good land. I am going to send you to bring them out."

Moses said, "Who am I to do that? Remember, I tried that when I was still a prince in Egypt. It didn't work."

God told him, "Yes, but you did it on your own; you didn't ask for my help. This time, I will be with you and I will do it. When you come out of Egypt, you are to worship me on this mountain."

Moses said, "Who shall I say is sending me? What is your name?"

God said, "I AM THAT I AM. Tell the people I AM sent you. That is my name, forever. I AM the God of their fathers, Abraham, Isaac, and Jacob."

Moses was to take a delegation and go to Pharaoh and tell him that God wanted them to go into the desert three days to sacrifice to him. God said Pharaoh would not let them go, but God would stretch out his hand and strike Egypt with His wonders, and finally Pharaoh would let them go. When he did, every woman was to borrow jewels and clothes from the Egyptians before they left, so they would have payment for their work of many years.

Moses, said, "They won't believe me or listen to me. They won't believe that you have told me to do this."

God said, "What is that in your hand?"

Moses said, "A rod"

God told him. "Throw it down on the ground."

When he did, it became a huge serpent. Moses ran away from it. The Lord told him to pick it up by the tail. When he did, it became a rod, again. Then He had Moses put his hand in his cloak. He did, and when he pulled it out, it was white with leprosy, an incurable disease. He put it back and it was clear again. God said that those were to be signs to the Israelites and to Pharaoh. Then he told Moses he was to turn the water in the river to blood as another sign.

Moses argued with God that he wasn't a good speaker, so he couldn't do what God was telling him to do. Actually, he was scared to even try it. He knew Egypt and how they all thought and acted. It was an impossible task!

God finally got rather angry with him and told him that he could take his brother, Aaron, with him to do the talking, but he would be the one God would speak to.

Moses went to Jethro and told him that he needed to go back to Egypt and see his family. Jethro told him, "Go in peace."

God told Moses that all the people who had tried to kill him were dead so he would be safe. Moses took his wife and his son and set off for Egypt, with the rod of God in his hand. God warned him that even after he had done all the wonders God had given him to do, Pharaoh would not believe him; but God would get them out with a mighty hand.

Moses had not circumcised his son, so Zipporah did it on the way. She did not understand, or approve of it at all, but she did it anyway to save Moses, who thought he could do God's will without obeying his covenant.

Trials of Egypt

God told Aaron, Moses' brother, to go into the wilderness to meet Moses---that he was on his way home. Aaron went.

Moses told Aaron all that God had told him to do. They went back to Egypt and told the people what God was going to do. The people believed and worshipped God. Moses and Aaron went to Pharaoh and told him what God had said to tell him.

Pharaoh's answer was, "Who is the Lord, that I should obey his word? I don't know him, and I won't let Israel go! Why are you keeping the people from their work?" Pharaoh was angry and commanded that slaves would no longer be given straw to make bricks. They must find their own straw, but they must make just as many bricks as if they had been given straw. Then the men were beaten because they didn't make enough bricks. Pharaoh said they had too much time on their hands and that was why they wanted to go into the desert and sacrifice to their god.

Moses went to God and complained that nothing was happening, except evil, since he came. God promised him that it would happen, but it would take God's mighty hand. He reminded Moses that He had promised Canaan land to Abraham, Isaac, and Jacob, and He was going to keep his promise.

Moses tried to tell the people, but they couldn't hear him because of the cruelty of their taskmasters.

God said, "Go to Pharaoh again."

Moses said, "The people won't listen to me. How can I expect Pharaoh to listen to me?"

God said, "Go anyway. Pharaoh holds you in great respect, but he won't do what you say, yet. They believe their gods are in charge of rain, thunder, fertility, crops growing and power. I am going to show these Egyptians who is really God. Take your rod and show the miracle I had you do in the desert."

So Moses and Aaron went and threw down his rod before Pharaoh. It became a serpent. The magicians of Pharaoh did the same with their rods. But Moses' serpent ate up all of their serpents. Pharaoh would not let the people go.

The next morning, Moses and Aaron met Pharaoh by the river. (Egyptians thought that Pharaoh made the sun rise and the rivers flow). Moses hit the water with his rod, and the WATER TURNED TO BLOOD in front of Pharaoh. All the waters in Egypt turned to blood. The fish died and the river began to stink. But the magicians were able to turn water to blood, too. Pharaoh didn't budge in his thinking or let the people go. A whole week passed.

Moses went to Pharaoh again and told him that this time he would bring FROGS upon the nation. There would be frogs everywhere, even in their beds! The magicians were able to produce frogs, too. But soon Pharaoh begged Moses to wave his rod and make the frogs disappear. Then he would let the people go. All the frogs died, but they left a terrible stink. They had to be shoveled up and burned.

As soon as the frogs were gone, Pharaoh changed his mind and would not let the people go. So Moses stretched out his rod and LICE covered the land. The magicians tried to do the same thing, but they could not make lice! Lice were on man and beast.

The magicians realized and told Pharaoh, "This is the finger of God doing this." Pharaoh wouldn't listen to them.

The next morning, Moses met Pharaoh again at the water. He told him that FLIES would be in all of Egypt, except this time, they would not be in the land of Goshen where God's people were; only on the Egyptians! (Imagine trying to tell a fly what to do and where to go! But God did!)

Pharaoh told him to sacrifice there in Egypt; but Moses said their God would not like that, and neither would the Egyptians.

Pharaoh asked Moses to beg for God to take away the flies. He said that they could go three days into the desert, but they were not to go very far. As soon as the flies were gone, Pharaoh changed his mind, again.

Next, all the LIVESTOCK of Egypt got a DISEASE AND DIED; none of the Israelites' livestock did. That just made Pharaoh angry.

Then God commanded Moses to throw dust into the air, and it became BOILS on people and animals. The magicians couldn't even stand before Pharaoh, because of their boils.

Next it was HAIL---except in Goshen, where the Israelites lived.

That was followed by LOCUSTS. That really upset Pharaoh. He said they could go with their children, but couldn't take their livestock. Moses would not agree to that, so Pharaoh changed his mind, again. He was so angry that he told Moses never to come back- -or he would die.

Moses told Pharaoh, "Fine. There is just one more plague God is going to call down on Egypt, so that all Egypt, with your many gods, will know there is just one God and it is He who is dealing with you! At midnight, He will go through all the land of Egypt and KILL ALL THE FIRSTBORN OF EVERY FAMILY, from Pharaoh, to the animals. There will be such a great outcry that Pharaoh and his people will push us out of the country."

God told Moses to tell his people to be prepared. They were to borrow everything they could from their Egyptian masters, and to be ready to go. The Egyptians gave them everything they asked for.

God told Moses that every family was to get a one-year-old lamb for their household, enough for each person in the family. It must be a perfect lamb, not a reject. They were to get it on the same day, and to kill the lamb on the same day, take the blood of that lamb and paint it on the side posts and the upper door post of the houses where they would be eating. They were to roast it whole, along with unleavened bread and bitter herbs, and eat it all. No one was to leave the house. They were to be dressed, ready to travel, with their shoes on, and their staff in their hands. When the angel of death saw the blood on their door posts, he would pass over their houses, and they would be safe.

They were to remember to do this, every year, for a week, from now on, as a memorial to God for what He had done for them. They were to call it "The Passover," because the angel of God had passed over them when he killed the Egyptians. That is exactly what the people did.

When the angel of death came into Egypt, there was not an Egyptian household that didn't have someone dead. There was a great outcry in all of Egypt. Pharaoh sent word to Moses and Aaron in the middle of the night. He told them to get out quick before all of Egypt died! To take everything they had and all their people. Just GET OUT!

So they left. They went from Raamses to Succoth. Moses and about six hundred thousand men, besides women and children, left Egypt, carrying their yeast and flour on their heads, because the bread didn't have time to rise. They took all their livestock and everything they could carry in carts, and on foot. It was exactly 430 years that they had been in Egypt, but God brought them out just as He said He would. Moses had them bring the bones of Joseph along with them and keep their promise to him.

Moses told the people that from now on, every firstborn male was to be special to the Lord, both man and animal. They were to buy it back with a sacrifice to God.

God didn't let the people go the direct route to Canaan. Instead he led them through the wilderness of the Red Sea, because God knew that they would be too afraid to fight the Philistines and would go back to Egypt. So they went from Succoth and camped in Etham on the edge of the wilderness.

God led them with a pillar of cloud in the daytime. At night, the pillar of cloud became a "Night Light," a pillar of fire, so they could see where they were going and know that God was with them continually.

God told Moses to camp between Migdol and the sea. He said, "Pharaoh will hear where you are. He will think you are trapped there and will follow you." Moses did as he was told.

Pharaoh came after them with 600 choice chariots, to bring back his slaves. The people were terrified when they saw Pharaoh coming. They cried out to God. God moved the pillar of cloud between them and Pharaoh's army. On Pharaoh's side it was dark; but on Israel's side was the fire to give light.

God told Moses, "Lift up your rod over the sea and divide it." The waters piled up on each side and left a dry path through the middle. A wind blew and held the waters there. All night the people of Israel passed through the sea on dry ground, with a wall of water on each side of them.

In the morning, the Egyptians tried to do the same thing; but their chariot wheels bogged down. Then, Moses stretched his rod over the waters and the waters all came flooding back. The Egyptians were drowned in the sea.

Moses and his sister, Miriam, led the people in a great song of celebration to the Lord for saving them and delivering them from the hand of Pharaoh and from slavery.

So, they went out into the wilderness of Shur, that whole great company of former slaves, now freed and on their way to Canaan.

Desert Training

The people of Israel went three days out into the wilderness. They came to an oasis and thought they would all have water; but the water was bitter. They named the place Marah (which means, "bitter").

They all began to murmur and complain against Moses. The Lord showed Moses a tree. When he had thrown it into the water the water became sweet.

They went on from there and found an oasis that had twelve wells of water, with forty palm trees. They camped there for a long time.

After a month and a half, they went into the desert. The whole group began to fuss at Moses because they didn't have enough food. They were even saying that it would have been better to die in Egypt than to be out in this desert and go hungry.

God told Moses that he was going to feed them. He would give them meat. The next night quail flew into the camp and covered the ground. God said that in the morning He would rain down bread from Heaven on them. Every morning, they were to go out and pick up the amount their family could eat in a day. If there was any left over at the end of the day, they were to throw it out. On the sixth day, they were to get twice as much, because there would not be any on the Sabbath day.

Like God said, along with the morning dew, little round things lay on the ground. The people called it manna, which means "What is it?" because they didn't know what it was. Moses told them. "This is the food God promised you. Pick it up and eat it."

They did. They could do anything with the manna; they could cook it, boil it, bake it, or eat it raw. There was nothing they could do to make it fall. They had to depend on God to give it to them every morning. But some of them didn't trust God to deliver it the next day and tried to keep the leftovers. It got worms in it and stank.

So when the Sabbath came, they were afraid to get enough to keep over, like the Lord had told them to, so they went hungry the next day, because there was no manna on the Sabbath.

God was trying to teach them obedience. They were slow learners! God told them they were to rest on the Sabbath day. When the cloud stopped, they did, too.

As they journeyed on, they found themselves in a place where there was no water. The people were so angry with Moses they were about to stone him.

Everything was always Moses' fault! They thought Moses was the one who was doing all this for them. They could see him, but they couldn't see God.

God told Moses to take some of the elders with him, take his rod, and when he came to a certain rock, he was to strike the rock with his rod. Water would come out of the rock. Moses did as God directed, and God gave them water from the rock.

Then came the Amalekites. They were going to fight with Israel to keep them from passing through their land.

Moses told Joshua to pick out men to fight, and Moses would go stand on the top of the hill, with the rod of God in his hand. He took Aaron and Hur with him to the top of the hill to watch the battle.

Joshua went to fight. As long as Moses held his hands up, the Israelites won; but when he let his hands down they began to lose. So, Aaron and Hur sat Moses down on a rock. They each took a hand and held it up. They held his hands up all day and the Amalekites were defeated. With God's help, Israel had won their first battle.

Moses' father in law, Jethro, heard that Moses was in the area with all the slaves of Egypt he had brought out of slavery. He came to see Moses and brought his daughter, Zipporah, Moses' wife, and his two sons back to Moses where they were camped in the Wilderness.

Moses told Jethro all that God had done for them. Jethro was very impressed with Moses' God, who showed up all of Egypt's gods in such a mighty way!

The next morning, Jethro watched as Moses sat all day settling the arguments of the people. He asked Moses about it. Then he gave Moses some very good advice. He told him, "Nobody can stand up under all this pressure. You need to pick good, honest men to help you rule over hundreds and thousands. You teach the people laws and rules, but let them bring only the hardest cases to you. Then you will be able to get this people into Canaan like God planned."

Moses was wise. He listened to his father-in-law and did as he suggested. They traveled on, until they came to the mountain where God had told Moses he was to come and worship.

The Mountain of God

God had told Moses that when he had brought all the people of Israel out of Egypt, he was to bring them to this mountain; so, now, that was where Moses and the people were, at the foot of the mountain.

God spoke to the people and told them that He loved them. He wanted to live with them. He wanted them to be a special people: His true followers, a holy nation, a royal priesthood, who would tell all the nations about their wonderful God, who did marvelous things for them. He reminded them of what He had done in bringing them out of slavery.

The people said, "Yes, we will do whatever God says."

Moses told the people to clean themselves up, wash their clothes and be ready, because in three days, God would come down in a thick cloud and talk to them. They were not to go up on the mountain where God was, or even touch it. But when the trumpet sounded, they were to come near the foot of the mountain and listen to God speak to them.

In the morning, when the trumpet sounded, there was thunder and lightning and a thick cloud on the mountain. When God talked to them, the people were scared to death. The people told Moses, "You talk to us, but don't have God talk to us. You tell us what He says. We are afraid of God."

God called to Moses and told him to come up to the top of the mountain. Moses went up and God talked to him.

God told Moses to tell the people, "You saw what I did to Pharaoh when he wouldn't listen to me. You saw how I carried you like an eagle carries her young. If you will obey my voice and keep my covenant, you will be a special people to me."

Then he gave Moses ten commandments to teach the people. It was God's way of showing the people how to live, safely. God wrote them on stone tablets. Here is what they said:

1. YOU SHALL HAVE NO OTHER GODS BEFORE ME.

2. YOU SHALL NOT MAKE ANY GRAVEN IMAGES, OR WORSHIP THEM.

3. YOU SHALL NOT TAKE THE NAME OF THE LORD YOUR GOD IN VAIN.

4. REMEMBER THE SABBATH DAY TO KEEP IT HOLY.

5. HONOR YOUR FATHER AND YOUR MOTHER.

6. YOU SHALL NOT KILL.

7.   YOU SHALL NOT COMMIT ADULTERY.

8.   YOU SHALL NOT STEAL.

9.   YOU SHALL NOT BEAR FALSE WITNESS.
      (LIE ABOUT ANYBODY)

10. YOU SHALL NOT COVET.

Each one of the covenant makers should have taken one of the tablets, but God gave both covenant tablets to Moses to put in the tabernacle where He planned to live in their camp with them.

God also gave Moses many other rules for the people to live by. They needed them because they had been slaves all their lives and just did what their masters had told them to do. Now they had to be able to think and live for themselves, and they needed to know how to do it.

Many of our laws today are still based on those same laws, when it comes to deciding who is right and who is wrong.

Moses took Joshua part way up the mountain with him, but Joshua didn't go into the cloud with Moses. God talked to Moses about a place where He could live among them. He told him exactly how to make it and what to use, making it. He called it an ark. He also told Moses how to prepare a tent tabernacle for the ark and what should go in it.

He told Moses just how they were to worship him, and that Aaron and his sons were to be His priests. He told him what their robes were to be like, what their sacrifices were to be, and how to offer them.

God said that He would live among the people and be their God. They would be His special people, to tell all the world about His goodness and His love. God even told Moses who was to do the work He was telling him to do. It took a long time for God to tell all this to Moses.

Down below, the people got antsy. They were used to Egyptian gods they could see and touch with their hands, like the Egyptians had. They went to Aaron and told him to make a god for them, because they didn't know what had happened to Moses.

Aaron tried to stop them, but they wouldn't listen. So, he had them bring their gold to him. He fashioned it into a calf, burnt it in fire, and set it up on an altar. The next day, they had a feast day, a day of debauchery, and many worshipped the golden calf.

God saw what they were doing. He told Moses to get back down the mountain. So, Moses and Joshua went back down the mountain to the camp.

Lessons

God knew what Moses would think when he saw what the people were doing, so God had said to Moses while he was still on the mountain before Moses saw the people, their debauchery, and their calf, "Let me kill this whole bunch and start over and raise up a nation from your children."

But Moses had realized that would make God look bad. He said, "The people of the world will say you were not able to take these people into Canaan like you promised, so you killed them in the wilderness."

God agreed, and let Moses tend to the people.

When Moses got down and saw what they were doing, he was furious. He threw down the tablets with the Ten Commandments on them, and they broke. Moses ground the calf into powder, put the powered gold in the water, and made the people drink it.

Moses yelled to all of them, "Who is on the Lord's side? Come here to me." All Levi's sons came. Moses told them to go all through the camp and kill every man who had a part in this rebellion against God. They killed about 3,000 men.

Moses had a meeting with God and begged Him to forgive the people.

God said He would. God also said, "These people are such a stubborn people, that I won't go with them any longer. If I do, I might kill them on the way when they refuse to listen to me and obey."

Moses told God, "If you don't go with us, how will anybody know that you are our God? If you don't go, I won't go, either."

So, God said, "Yes, I will forgive them, again, and go with you."

Moses begged to see God's face. God told him, "No one can see my face and live; but I will put you in a little cave and as I pass by, I will cover your face with my hand, then remove it so you can see my backside."

Moses was to make two stone tablets like God had made, bring them up to the mountain, and God would write on them, again. So he did.

God promised to drive out all the people who were now living in Canaan and give the land to Israel. He would forgive their sin and be their God.

Moses was up on the mountain 40 days and 40 nights, without eating or drinking. When Moses came down from the mountain and the presence of God, the skin of his face shone with the Glory of God. It frightened the people, so they were afraid to come near him. So, he put a veil over his face. When he went into the tabernacle to talk with the Lord, he took off the veil. When he came back out, he put it back on.

He had the people build the ark and the tabernacle just as God had told him on the mountain. He set everything up just as God had told him to do. When it was all finished, the Glory of God came down and filled the tabernacle. The cloud that had led them settled down on the tabernacle.

When the pillar of cloud moved, the people got up and followed it. When the cloud settled down on the tabernacle, the people camped and stayed until the cloud moved, again. They didn't know when they were going, where they were going or when they were stopping. They just followed the cloud of God.

God told Moses exactly how He was to be worshipped. He had Moses count all the people and do a genealogy on them.

He told Moses exactly how the priesthood should work, all about the sacrifices, how they were to live holy unto Him, how their sins could be forgiven and the conditions for God to bless them. It took a long time.

As the people traveled on into the wilderness, they again complained about not having meat to eat. They complained about the manna God was providing--it didn't have the flavor of onions, and leeks, and garlic.

God was displeased with them, and Moses was anguished over them. He couldn't give them the food they'd had in Egypt because they were out in the desert!

They still blamed Moses and God. Moses told God that he couldn't do it alone, so God had him select seventy "God anointed" men to help him.

In answer to their fussing, God told Moses to tell the people they were going to have meat, not just for a day, or a week, but for a solid month, until they were sick of it. God sent a wind, and it blew in so many quail that the ground was stacked two feet high with them for miles around on all sides of the camp. Of course, there was no refrigeration in the desert. The people got sick because they kept eating them long after they should have quit.

Miriam didn't like Moses' foreign wife. She talked Aaron into complaining against her, too, saying that God had spoken to them as well as Moses. She said that Moses wasn't the only one to lead the people. God heard them. He called Moses, Aaron, and Miriam to all come out before the tabernacle in front of the people.

God told the people, "Moses is my chosen prophet. How dare any of you speak against him?!"

When the cloud left the tabernacle, Miriam was white as snow from leprosy. Moses and Aaron were shocked at what God had done to her. Moses begged God to make her well, again.

God told him. "If her father had been angry with her and spit in her face, she would be ashamed for seven days; so, put her out of the camp for a week. Then she will be well and can come back."

So, the entire camp stayed there until Miriam was well and could come back with a different attitude.

They were a long time in the desert, getting the laws and building the tabernacle. Finally they came to the wilderness of Paran and camped there.

God told Moses to pick a man from every tribe to send as spies into Canaan land to see what it was like, before they went in to conquer the land. So Moses did.

The men were gone for forty days. When they came back, they brought huge branches covered with grapes so heavy it took two of them to carry. They also brought back figs and pomegranates. They showed the people the fruit of the land, but they said, "The walls are high, and the people are huge---giants! We aren't able to overcome them."

Caleb, and Joshua, who had also gone as spies, told the people, "Let's go right away and win this place. We are well able to do it. God will help us!"

The people only listened to the other spies.

All that night, all the people wept and wailed and said that they wouldn't go. "It would have been better for us to have died in Egypt than to come out here and face these giants! Let's choose a captain and go back to Egypt!"

Moses, Joshua, and Caleb, tore their clothes in anguish, and pleaded with the people. They tried to tell them that God was with them, and He would make them successful, but, it was no use. The people were ready to stone them.

Then the Glory of the Lord appeared on the tabernacle in front of all the people. God was angry with them! He said, "After all I have done for you and all the miracles I have shown you, you still don't listen or obey me."

He was ready to kill the whole nation, and start over with Moses.

Moses begged for the people, again, and God spared their lives. But God declared, "All those men who have seen all my miracles and yet rebelled, from twenty years old and upwards, will NOT get to go into Canaan. They will all die in the wilderness. Only faithful Caleb and Joshua will get to go in."

The next morning, the whole camp decided they would go, after all. They tried, but they lost the battle, badly. Their disobedience sent them back into the wilderness. They were in the desert for forty years.

Desert Adventures

Even though God was furious with His people, He still cared for them. As they wandered in the wilderness, He kept their shoes and their clothes from wearing out. He fed them manna every day.

Now, some of the Levite priests decided they should be leading the people, instead of Moses. They were blaming Moses for not getting them into Canaan, even though they knew it was the people's fault. They just wanted the power Moses had.

Their names were Korah, Dathan and Abiram. Moses called them all out to stand before God at the tabernacle so God could show the people who was in charge. God opened up the earth, and it swallowed all the rebels and their families and their belongings.

The next day, the congregation murmured against Moses because they said that he had killed the people of the Lord. (As if he could cause an earthquake!)

God was so angry with them that He started to wipe out the whole mess with a plague. Moses and Aaron fell on their faces before God. Then Moses had Aaron take fire off the altar in a censer and run among the people. Aaron stood between the dead and the living and the plague was stopped. About 14,000 died in the plague.

God was sick of their fighting for place. He had Moses have every tribe bring a rod with their name on it to the house of the Lord, to show who was to be God's priest. All of the rods were left in the tabernacle. God said that the rod of the man He chose would blossom and he didn't want to hear any more complaints from them after that! Twelve rods were put into the tabernacle, one per tribe.

The following day, Moses brought out all the rods. They looked, and every man took his rod. Aaron's rod had budded, bloomed blossoms, and had even yielded almonds! God had appointed Aaron and his tribe to be priests forever over the house of Israel. They alone were to serve at the Tabernacle before the Lord. They were not to inherit any of the land in Canaan, but were to be cared for by the offerings of the people as they gave offerings to God.

The next trial to Moses came when the people again complained. This time it was about the manna. They said they hated it.

God sent fiery serpents among them. They bit people and they died. The people came to Moses and said they were sorry they had offended him and God, and to please pray for them. Moses did.

God told him to make a fiery serpent out of brass and put it up on a tall pole in the middle of the camp. If anyone got bitten, he was to look at the serpent of brass and God would heal him. Everyone who believed God was healed and didn't die.

They fought several battles with the people around them who would not let them pass. God helped them win their battles.

They came to the cities of Balak. Balak sent to a man named Balaam, who was called a "man of God." He wanted Balaam to curse the Israelites for him. He sent a lot of money to Balaam to bribe him to come and curse them. Balaam had the men wait until morning, so he could pray about it.

That night, God told Balaam, "Do not go. I am blessing these people. You are not to curse them."

The king sent more men and promised Balaam anything he wanted if he would come. The temptation was too great; finally, he went with them. But as they were on the way, God sent his angel to kill Balaam.

He was riding a little donkey and had his two servants with him. The donkey saw the angel and wouldn't go toward the angel. It turned into a field instead. Balaam beat the donkey.

They went back onto the road, but the angel had moved to where there was a wall on each side. The donkey crushed Balaam's foot against the wall, trying to escape the angel.

Next, the angel went to a place where there was no turning around. The donkey lay down. Balaam was angry and beat her.

God let the donkey talk and tell Balaam why she had done these things, and scold him for beating her.

God opened Balaam's eyes, and he saw the angel and realized that his donkey had saved his life. He was sorry he had beaten her.

The angel told Balaam to go with the men, but to say only what God told him to say when he got there.

Balak made an offering on the top of the hill. But when he asked Balaam to curse the Israelites as they passed by, Balaam could only bless them, instead. Three times he blessed them. Balak was furious. He told Balaam to go home without any payment.

Balaam foretold that "THERE SHALL COME A STAR OUT OF JACOB, AND A SCEPTER SHALL RISE OUT OF ISRAEL. (Centuries later, the wise men followed the star to find the baby Jesus).

Almost There

God had Moses take another census to see if all the people who were not allowed to go into Canaan were dead. They found that not one was left. Forty years and eleven months after they had left Egypt, Moses told the people that they had been long enough in this desert. It was time to go into Canaan land and possess it. They started for Canaan.

Moses allotted the land to the men of the different families. One family had only daughters. There were five of them. They came to Moses and told him that their father had not been in the rebellion. Why should his name be blotted out because he had no sons?

Moses asked God about it, and God told him to give their father's inheritance to his daughters, and from now on, if a man had only daughters, his inheritance was to go to his daughters. If there were no children, the inheritance would go to his brothers; then, other relatives.

They ran into the Midianites. The children of Israel went to war with the Midianites. They conquered all that land.

When the sons of Gad and Reuben and half the tribe of Manasseh saw how good the land was for cattle, they went to Moses and asked him to let them settle there. Moses was displeased with them for even suggesting it. It was too much like what their fathers had done in refusing to go in, 40 years ago.

The men told Moses that they wouldn't inherit, over in Canaan. What they wanted to do was build sheep folds on the east side of the Jordan River, and when it came time to go into Canaan, they were willing to leave their livestock and families and go at the head of all the soldiers. They would fight with the Canaanites until everyone had found his inheritance; then they would return to their homes on the east side of the Jordan.

Once they explained what they planned, Moses said it would be all right. So they built cities and sheepfolds and prepared to settle there on that side of the river.

God told Moses to go up into the mountain. He was going to show Moses all the land of Canaan. Then Moses was going to die.

He was not going to be allowed to go into Canaan, because back in the desert of Zin, Moses had disobeyed God. Moses had been mad at the people again. This time he was very angry because they were blaming him again for the lack of water.

God had told Moses to go to a certain place where there was a rock. He was to speak to the rock and water would come out. Moses was so mad at the people that instead of speaking to the rock, he struck the rock with his rod.

Moses asked God about a leader for His people. God told him to anoint Joshua, the son of Nun, to be leader in his place. God said that He had put His spirit in Joshua. So, Moses took Joshua before all the people and the priests, and anointed him and charged him to be the new leader, after himself.

Moses reminded all the people and the priests of all the laws, the sacrifices, and everything they needed to know as a nation. He spent a long time telling them and preparing them to go into Canaan.

Moses had kept a log of all the places they had been and all the laws God had given them. He reminded them that they were to utterly destroy all the people in the places they conquered; because if they left them, they would start to worship their gods and fall away from the Lord their God.

He reminded them of all the miracles God had done for them. Though these people had not seen them, their parents had. He reminded them of all the failures of the people; times when they had grumbled, and then refused to go into the land, when God had said to go. Moses told them not to ever do that, again! He reminded them that they were a HOLY PEOPLE. They were supposed to act like it!

He told them, "The Eternal God is your refuge, and underneath are the everlasting arms."

Moses was 120 years old when he climbed up Mount Nebo. He could still see well. He was still strong. He was still following the Lord. But he knew, and God knew, that the people needed a new, young leader to take them into Canaan. The road would be hard and long. It was time for Moses to have a rest.

From the mountain, God showed Moses all the land of Canaan and told him where each tribe was to live.

So Moses, the servant of the Lord, died there in the land of Moab on the mountain and God buried him. No one knows where his grave is. The whole company mourned in the plains of Moab for thirty days for Moses There was not a prophet before or after like Moses, whom the Lord knew face to face. The miracles God did through Moses will always be remembered.

Moses served his God and his people. HE WAS A REAL HERO!

Joshua was a hero. Not the same kind as Moses, because that was not the kind God needed, now. Joshua was a soldier. He knew how to fight battles and win. He had been with Moses on the mountain, in the Tabernacle and when he faced the angry people so many times. He had always stood fast by Moses' side and helped him; but taking over must have terrified him.

Young folks today have somewhat the same problem when they have a very famous father--how do you live up to it? But Joshua did, and became a real hero.

Though it seems harsh to us, Israel is symbolic. God is trying to show us how to deal with sin. He tells us to utterly destroy it. Not to keep some little pet sins in our lives, because they will grow up to be giant monsters that will destroy us. The Hebrews were to destroy all the people with their gods, so they would not be tempted to follow strange gods.

When they obeyed, they succeeded. When they didn't, they failed, and got sucked into the false religions of those they had left around them.

It eventually caused their downfall. It always pays to follow God's direction, and learn from the mistakes of others.

Joshua

Moses was dead. Now it was up to Joshua to lead the people of Israel. God had appointed him in Moses' place. I think Joshua was scared to death, because God kept telling him to be strong and of a great courage.

Joshua had seen all that Moses had gone through, trying to get these people into Canaan and keep them following God.

When Moses went up the mountain, nobody but Joshua was to even touch the mountain. Joshua went part way up with Moses. When Moses went into the tent to worship God, Joshua had sat in the corner and listened to him talking with God.

Now Joshua had to do the talking with God, himself. Joshua was a man of war. Talking wasn't his way of doing things, but he had to learn to talk, and especially to listen.

God told Joshua to take the people over the Jordan River into Canaan land. He promised Joshua that just as He had been with Moses, He would be with Joshua. Joshua believed God.

Joshua told the people to get ready, because in three days they would cross the river to take the land which God had given them. Joshua sent out two spies to spy out the land. He sent them into Jericho, the city right across the river from where they were encamped.

The two men were clearly strangers to the people of Jericho, so they were spotted. There was a house on the wall. It belonged to a prostitute named Rahab. Rahab urged the men to come into her house. They went.

The king of Jericho sent men to Rahab's house to arrest them but Rahab hid the men under some flax stalks on her roof. She sent the soldiers on a made-up story of how the men had escaped. She kept the men there until morning. In the morning, she told them that all of Jericho was terrified of the God of the Hebrews. They had all heard how He opened the Red Sea and led them through, 40 years ago, and how He had fought their battles, ever since.

She believed in their God. She asked the men to save her life and the lives of her family when they captured Jericho.

The men made a deal with Rahab. Since she helped them escape, she and all of her family were to be spared when the war came.

Rahab let the men down over the side of the wall with a red rope. She told them to go hide for three days before going back to their camp, which they did.

They agreed that she would have that same rope hanging from her window over the wall on the day of the battle, so all would know where she was, and whom to save.

Rahab had absolutely no training about Israel's God, but she saw His power. She believed that He was truly God and could do anything He wanted to do. Her faith saved her and her family. Rahab was a hero.

Joshua told the people, "When you see the Ark of the Covenant with the priests carrying it, move out. You are to follow it, but leave a space between you and it."

He told the priests, "Pick up the Ark and go ahead of the people. Go and stand in the middle of the Jordan River. As soon as your feet touch the water, the water will dry up and the people can go over the Jordan on dry ground, because our God, the God of all the earth, is with us. It doesn't make any difference that the river is at flood stage. It is a sign that God is going to fight our battles for us and with us."

All the people passed over on dry ground. God had told Joshua to choose twelve men, one from each tribe. They were to go into the river and pick up twelve stones, carry them over into Canaan and pile them up where they were to camp that night. Then He had them each carry a stone and put it into the river where the priests had stood. The stones were to be a memorial to all generations of what the Lord had done for them in drying up the river so they could go over on dry ground.

When everything was accomplished, Joshua told the priests to come out of the water. When they came out, the water returned to its place and again overflowed the river.

The people believed God, and had respect for Joshua, just like they had for Moses.

When the people of the land heard about God drying up the river so that hundreds of thousands of men, besides women and children and animals, could pass over on dry ground, they were terrified. They were afraid to come near the camp of Israel.

The Lord told Joshua to circumcise all the men, because they had not circumcised any in the wilderness. They celebrated the Passover and began to eat the food that grew around them. The manna stopped coming, then.

Joshua was walking by Jericho one evening when he saw a man with a drawn sword in his hand. Joshua went up to him and asked him, "Are you for us, or for our enemies?"

The man answered, "No, but, as captain of the Host of the Lord, I have come." (I'm not taking sides; I've come to take over!)

Joshua fell down and worshipped and said to him, "What do you have to say to me, your servant?"

The captain told Joshua to take off his shoes because the place where he was standing was Holy. (Start with worship). Joshua did so.

All the walls of Jericho were shut tightly and no one went in or out. They were scared to death.

The Lord told Joshua, "I have given Jericho to you, with its king and all its mighty men." Then He gave Joshua a strange battle plan.

The armed men were to go, first. Next were to come seven priests, blowing seven trumpets, continually. Then the priests carrying the Ark of the Covenant were to come, followed by other armed men. Then all the people were to bring up the rear. They were to march around the city once each day without making a sound, except for the trumpets. On the seventh day, they were to march around seven times. On the seventh time, the trumpets were to blast loudly, the people were to shout, and the walls would fall down flat.

That is exactly what they did, and that is what happened. When the people shouted, the walls fell down flat and the soldiers walked over the flat walls into Jericho. God had done it all.

They destroyed everything. Only the gold, silver, brass and iron were to go into the treasury. Everything else was to be destroyed.

Joshua sent the two spies, who had been saved by Rahab, to her house, the only place on the walls that didn't fall down, to bring her and her family out to safety.

Rahab lived with the Israelites from then on. She married one of them and became an ancestor of King David and of the Christ. God honored her faith. Rahab was a hero.

Tricks

Now when the people who lived in Gibeon heard what Joshua had done to Jericho and Ai, they made a plan to save themselves.

They pretended to be people from a far away land who had heard of the things Israel's God had done and who wanted to make peace with Israel.

The men put on old, raggedy clothes and worn-out shoes, got moldy bread and wine, and put old sacks on their donkeys.

They went to Joshua's camp and told them, "We had all new stuff when we left home, but it was such a long journey to get here that it has all worn out."

Joshua and the leaders believed them and made an agreement with them before God, that they would live in peace. Joshua did not ask the Lord about it, first. But, in a few days, the whole camp found out that the Gibeonites had lied. They lived a short distance away from them in Canaan. But because of their pact before the Lord, the Israelites could not destroy them, as they were supposed to and had planned.

So, they made them workers for the Israelites, forever. They were to carry the water and cut the wood. They became slaves, but they had saved their lives.

They were a constant reminder of how important it is for God's people to check with God first before making decisions. The enemy can lie, but it is important for God's people to keep their word.

The kings of other cities around heard how the people of Gibeon had made peace with Joshua. They were angry. The five kings of the Amorites got together to wage war on Gibeon. Gibeon sent word to

Joshua to come and help them, so Joshua and all his army came. The Lord rained down hail stones on the armies of the enemies and killed more than were killed with the sword.

As they were fighting and winning the battle, they needed more time to completely defeat the enemy. In front of everybody, Joshua called to the sun to stand still and the moon to wait until the battle was over. The sun stopped moving and stayed where it was for an entire day, giving Joshua an extra day to win the battle he needed to win. God had answered his prayer for the extra time. There has been no day like it before or since, when God stretched out one day into two because his servant asked. When the long two days were over, all of Israel returned to their camp at Gilgal.

For years, Joshua fought all the cities and kings around him and won all his battles. Some cities they burned, but the great cities, they kept and lived in. They utterly destroyed everything God had told them to destroy.

They obeyed, but they had not taken all the land of Canaan. They still had not taken all the lands of the Philistines and the Geshurites.

Joshua was getting old. God told him to allot all the land to the various tribes so each one knew what was theirs, where they were to live, and whom they were to drive out. They drew by lots for their inheritance.

Caleb is another hero. He is a man who had the courage to fight the Lord's battle wherever he was. He did not give in to the problems he saw; instead, he trusted in the Lord to take them through whatever got in the way of doing God's will. Even in his old age, Caleb believed his God could make them victorious, and He did. He's a hero worth following.

Caleb

Then Caleb, the son of Jephunneh, came to Joshua. He reminded him of how he and Joshua had brought back the good report to Moses about going into the land, and how God had promised that only he and Joshua could go into Canaan.

He said, "I was forty years old at that time. Moses swore to me that the land where we had walked would be mine. Now, I want that land. The Lord has kept me alive. Now I am 85 years old, but, I am as strong now as I was that day. I am strong enough to go to war. NOW, THEREFORE GIVE ME THIS MOUNTAIN, where the Anakites were, where the cities were fenced and great, that the people were so afraid of. If the Lord will be with me, I will drive out those giants, as the Lord said."

So Joshua gave Caleb Hebron for an inheritance, because he followed the Lord God of Israel, completely.

Caleb captured three cities. When he came to the fourth, he told his men, "Whoever takes this city, I will give my daughter, Acsah, to him for a wife."

His nephew, Othniel, took it, so Acsah married Othniel. Acsah came to Caleb and asked for water springs to go with the field that he had given her. He granted her request.

So, Caleb proved what God had told them: that they didn't need to be afraid of giants, as long as the Lord their God was with them.

Joshua's Farewell

Joshua called the Reubenites, Gadites, and the half tribe of Manasseh and told them they had done very well in fighting for the land with the rest of Israel. Now they could go home to their families. He told them to be very careful to obey the laws that Moses had handed down to them. Even though they were on the other side of the Jordan River, they were still Israelites. They were to remember to love the Lord their God with all their hearts and walk in his ways.

The children of the two and a half tribes built an altar in the same fashion as the one built by Moses. They gave it a name: A Witness Between Us that the LORD is God. It was to be a reminder to future generations that they, too, were of the tribes of Israel, even though they lived across the river.

A long time later, the land was pretty much settled. Joshua was very old, and felt it. He called all the tribes together to come to him. He reminded them of all God had done for them, all they had done and all that had happened since they came into Canaan, how the Lord had blessed them, fought for them, and worked miracles for them.

He told them to not forget all the laws of Moses, to be careful to love the Lord their God. Joshua reminded them of what would happen to them if they began to worship the idols of the people around them. Joshua told them, "If it seems evil to you to serve the Lord, choose today whom you will serve, 'BUT AS FOR ME AND MY HOUSE, WE WILL SERVE THE LORD!'" And the people answered, "God forbid that we should forsake the Lord, to serve other gods."

Joshua died, being one hundred ten years old. They buried him in the border of his inheritance, in the hill country of Ephraim.

Judges

The people served God all the days of Joshua and all the days of the elders who lived longer than Joshua, who had seen the miracles that God did for them.

The armies kept driving out the enemy most of the time, but some of them did not drive out the people who lived there. They left them in the land, and instead of winning them to the Lord, they began to follow their gods.

When the old men who had seen the Lord's miracles died, the next generation didn't follow the Lord their God. Instead, they began to follow Baal and Ashtaroth, gods of the Canaanites, who still lived there.

God was angry with them. He no longer helped them drive out the enemy since they weren't serving Him. The enemy armed themselves and began to fight against Israel, just like God had said they would. They had a continuous battle with all those they had left in the country.

Israel no longer had anyone like Joshua to lead them, but God raised up various people to help them win their battles---people like Ehud and Shamgar. As long as these men lived, Israel followed God, but as soon as they died, they went after the idols of their neighbors.

God let them get into trouble. Then, when they called to Him, He sent another person to rescue them.

Deborah

Our first hero in the time of the Judges is Deborah. She seems to be the only one who had the courage to believe what God told her, and to lead her people into battle and victory. She far surpassed the men of her day.

A woman named Deborah was a prophetess and a judge at that time. She held court under a palm tree.

The enemy was Jabin, king of Canaan, whose captain was Sisera. Sisera had 900 chariots of iron. He mightily oppressed the Israelites. Deborah called a man named Barak to go and fight against Sisera. She told him to take 3,000 men, where and how to go, and that God would give him the victory. Barak said that he would only go if she went with him. So, she went, but she told Barak that the credit for the victory would go to a woman, which it did, because a woman, Jael, killed Sisera as he slept in her house.

God had delivered his people again.

Gideon

Gideon is another hero. He had the courage to believe God and follow his instructions exactly, even when it didn't make sense, and the wisdom to make sure it was God speaking to him. God used him to show His mighty power.

Again, the Children of Israel did evil in the sight of the Lord; and the Lord delivered them into the hands of Midian for seven years. As soon as the crops were ready to harvest, the Midianites would come and take everything: crops---even sheep, cattle and donkeys. The Israelites were very poor. They finally cried to the Lord for help.

The Lord sent an angel to talk to a man named Gideon. Gideon was threshing a bit of wheat, hiding behind a winepress so the Midianites wouldn't come and take what he had.

The angel said to him, "The Lord is with you, you mighty man of valor."

Gideon answered, "If the Lord is with us, why are we in such trouble with the Midianites?"

The angel told Gideon to go out and save his people because God had sent him.

Gideon said, "How can I save this people? My family is poor, and I am the least important in my father's house."

The angel told him, "God says that you can do it because I am with you."

Gideon asked the angel to stay while he got a present for him. The angel stayed, then burned up the food and drink Gideon brought him; so Gideon knew that it was an angel of God who had been speaking to him.

Gideon built an altar to God and worshipped him, there.

That night, God told Gideon to go up and take a seven-year-old bull to the hill top where his father had built an altar to Baal. He was to throw down Baal's altar, burn the grove around it, build an altar to the Lord and sacrifice the bull on it.

Gideon took ten men with him and did what God had commanded. They named Gideon, "Jerub-Baal," because he fought against Baal and put him down.

Gideon asked God for a sign. He put out a sheep skin. In the morning, if the dew was on the skin only, it meant God was sending him to battle. The next night, he asked for it to be reversed; a dry skin, with dew all around it.

God did both; so Gideon knew it was God telling him what to do.

The Midianites and Amalekites went to war against Israel. Gideon sent for all the fighting men to come to him. They came.

God told Gideon, "There are too many men; tell all who are afraid to go home." Twenty-two thousand went home. There were still ten thousand fighting men left for Gideon's army.

God said, "There are still too many. I want you to know that it is not you winning this battle, but I am the one who is giving you the victory."

God had Gideon bring all the men down to the river to drink water. All the ones who brought their hand to their mouth to drink, God selected to be in Gideon's army. All the others were sent home. There were only three hundred left.

Gideon was scared, so God sent him to spy out the enemy camp and listen to what they were saying. He heard a man telling of a dream he'd had. It told Gideon that God was going to give him the victory.

So Gideon divided his 300 men into three companies. He gave every man a trumpet and an empty pitcher, with lighted lamps in the pitchers. They were to surround the camp of the enemy. In the middle of the night, when Gideon blew his trumpet, they were each to blow their trumpets, break their pitchers so the lights shone, and shout, "The sword of the Lord and of Gideon!"

When they did as the Lord had told Gideon to do, it so startled and awoke the army of the enemy that they began to fight each other in the darkness, and to run away. All the other tribes and armies of Israel went out to chase after and defeat them as they ran toward home. The Israelites were delivered from their oppressors, again.

The people wanted to make Gideon their king; and his sons after him to be kings, but Gideon would have no part in it. He told them, "Worship the Lord your God. He is your King."

The people worshipped the Lord all the days of Gideon, but as soon as he died, they went back to worshipping Baal.

It was a constant pattern. As soon as the judge died, Israel went after other gods. They were despicable gods, and child sacrifice was often a requirement for worshipping them. God had told them they were never to put their children in the fire. Their children were sacred to Him. God was very upset at them.

Jephthah

Jephthah was another judge. He won battles, but he wasn't very wise. He was not really a hero; perhaps his daughter is the hero in this story.

This time it was the Ammonites who were oppressing Israel. God raised up a man named Jephthah.

Jephthah vowed to God that if God would let him win the battle, he would sacrifice to the Lord whatever first came out of his house to meet him when he got home.

God made him victorious. When he came home, the first one to come rushing out to meet her father was his only child, a daughter. She was so glad to see her father, but he was aghast. He hadn't counted on her being the one to greet him, first.

When he told her of his vow, her answer was, "My father, if you have made a vow to the Lord, you must keep it. Do to me whatever you promised to the Lord."

When she realized that she would never be allowed to marry and have children, she asked for permission to wander the countryside for two months with her friends, to mourn for her lack of children. She came back after the two months, and kept the vow.

Jephthah judged Israel for only six years. Then he died.

Several other judges came after him, but they didn't do much.

Samson

Samson was perhaps the physically strongest man to ever live. He had such potential, but he blew it by his lusts and foolishness. He finally got back to God and God honored him. Samson shows that we can waste our gifts and lose out with people and with God. I wouldn't call Samson a hero, neither is he a scoundrel, but you need to know about this strong man.

The children of Israel did evil again in the sight of the Lord, and the Lord delivered them to the Philistines for forty years.

There was a man and wife of the tribe of the Danites. They had no children because she couldn't have them. One day, the angel of the Lord appeared to the woman and told her that she was to have a son. She was not to drink any strong drink or eat anything unclean. Her son was never to cut his hair or drink strong drink, either. He was to be a Nazirite from birth.

The woman had a son. They named him Samson. He grew up, and God blessed him with great strength.

One day, Samson went down into the Philistine camp, Timnah, and saw a woman who pleased him. He told his father and mother to get her for him for a wife. His parents were displeased that he wanted a Philistine wife, but they did as he asked.

As they were going to Timnah to speak to her father, a lion sprang upon Samson. The Spirit of the Lord came upon him and he killed the lion, easily, without a weapon of any kind. He didn't tell his parents about it; they just continued on.

After some time, Samson went down to marry the girl. On the way, he went looking for the dead lion. When he found it, there was a swarm of bees and honey in the carcass of the lion. He reached in and took some of the honey and ate it.

When he got to Timnah, he made a wedding feast. At the feast, he made a riddle. He told them that if they could solve the riddle within the seven days of the feast, he would give them 30 changes of clothes and 30 linen garments. But, if they could not solve the riddle, they must give him the same. They agreed.

Then he told his riddle: "Out of the eater came something to eat; out of the strong came something sweet."

The men of Timnah tried for days to solve the riddle, but could not. On the seventh day, they went to Samson's wife and told her to find out what it was or they would burn her and her father's house down.

Samson's wife begged him to tell her the meaning of the riddle, pleading that he didn't love her if he didn't. Finally, he told her, and she told the men at the feast. Samson knew they had gotten it out of his wife.

His strength came upon him. He went down to a Philistine city and killed 30 men and took their stuff and paid the men at the feast with it. Samson was so angry! He went back to his father's house. Meanwhile, Samson's wife was given to another man, whom Samson had thought was his friend.

When Samson went down to get her, he was not allowed near her.

Samson was very angry with all of them. He went out and caught 300 foxes, tied their tails together, set fire to them, and turned them loose in the grain fields of the Philistines. They did a lot of damage, burning up shocks, grain fields and vineyards. The Philistines were so angry that they killed the girl and her father. Those were vicious times!

The Philistines went into Israel to get Samson. Samson killed many of them; then he went down into a cave in the rocks of Etam.

Three thousand men of Judah went to talk to Samson. Samson knew they wanted to turn him over to the Philistines. Samson made them promise they would not try to hurt him, themselves. He didn't want to hurt any of his own people. They promised not to do anything to him. He let them tie him up with new ropes and take him to the Philistines.

The Philistines shouted against him. The Spirit of the Lord came upon him and he burst the ropes as though they were nothing. He found the jaw bone of a donkey and killed a thousand Philistines with it. Afterward, he was thirsty and cried out to God, who provided water for him, miraculously.

Though Samson was exceedingly strong; he had a weakness for beautiful women, especially Philistine women, even though they were the enemy.

He went down to the camp of the Philistines again and saw a prostitute. He visited her. The Philistines heard that he was there. They surrounded the place all night, intending to kill him in the morning.

The city had high walls and the gates were shut, so they thought Samson was trapped. Samson got up at midnight to leave. When he got to the gates that were shut, he just pulled up the posts that held the gates of the city. He carried the gates and the posts up to the hill top and left them there. God was his strength.

Next, Samson fell in love with another Philistine woman, named Delilah. The Philistines heard of it. They came to her and told her, "If you will find out where his great strength comes from and how to stop him, we will each give you 1100 pieces of silver." Delilah agreed to the bargain.

When he came to visit her, Delilah begged Samson to tell her how he could lose his strength.

He told her that if he were tied with seven green vines, he would lose his strength. The Philistines were hiding in her house.

When Samson came to her, Delilah got him to fall asleep on her lap. While he was asleep, she tied him with vines the Philistines had brought her.

Then she woke Samson up, saying, "Samson! The Philistines are here and after you."

Samson jumped up, popped the vines as though they were nothing and ran off.

Next time he came, instead of accusing her, Samson listened to her whine about how he had tricked her! (HOW DUMB CAN YOU GET?!!)

She said, "You lied to me! Now tell me the truth!"

So, he told her another lie. He said that it was new ropes that would cause him to lose his strength.

She tried again, but the new ropes did nothing to hold Samson, either.

Next, he told her that if she wove the seven locks of his hair into a loom, he would lose his strength. She wove his hair into a loom and called the Philistines. He jumped up and went away with the pin of the beam and the whole loom.

Delilah accused him of not loving her and mocking her. She kept at it, day after day. Like a fool, he kept coming back.

Finally he told her the truth, He said, "I have been a Nazirite from birth. I have never had a razor on my head. If my hair is cut, I will lose my strength."

Delilah coaxed him to fall asleep on her knees again, and called the Philistines to come, once again. She said, "This time, I am sure."

She had someone cut his hair. (He sure must have been a sound sleeper). Then she woke him, saying, "Samson, wake up. The Philistines are here to get you."

Samson woke up and planned to run out as usual, but he didn't realize that Delilah had shaved his head, the Lord had left him and his strength was gone. The Philistines caught him and put out his eyes, tied him up and took him down to push the grinder in the prison house like a beast of burden. He stayed there a long time, but his hair began to grow out, again.

The Philistines had a great feast in a huge arena, held up by two giant posts. They called for Samson so they could jeer at him and at his God. They said their god had delivered Samson into their hands.

There were about 3,000 men and women on the roof of the place. All the lords of the Philistines were up there. They were all making fun of Samson's God, whom they said was powerless to save Samson.

Samson was still blind. He asked the boy who was bringing him in, to put him by the two central pillars holding up the building. The boy did as Samson asked.

Samson called to the Lord, "Oh, Lord, remember me! Strengthen me this one more time!

Then he leaned on the two support pillars with all his might and shouted out, "Let me die with the Philistines!" The whole building crashed to the ground.

So, Samson killed more in his death than he did in his life. Samson had judged Israel for twenty years.

I think God had the story of Samson put in the Bible to show us that even when we get ourselves into trouble, when we call on God, He will help us. I think God expects us to remember that with His help, we can pull up the gates of hell and carry them off, get ourselves out of the trap, and escape from addictions and sins. Others who want to can come out, too. It isn't our hair; it is the Spirit of God within us.

Ruth

Our next hero is a woman, a Moabite, a descendant of Lot. She didn't start out to try to be a hero. She just did the kind thing and followed the God she had learned to love, while living in her husband's family. Her faithfulness earned her a place in the lineage of King David and of Jesus.

This story happened in the time of the Judges.

A man named Elimelech, his wife, Naomi, and his two sons, Mahlon and Chilion, went to Moab to live, because there was a famine in Israel.

After awhile, Elimelech, Naomi's husband died. She raised her two sons and found wives for them from the girls of Moab. The name of one was Orpah. The other was named Ruth. They lived there about ten years. Then both of the sons died with no children.

It was a terrible thing to be a widow woman in those times, especially in a foreign land. A woman needed a husband or sons to take care of her. There were no jobs for women.

Naomi decided that she must go home to Israel. Her daughters-in-law were going to go with her but as they got started, Naomi thought better of it. She told the girls to go home to their mothers. They had been good to her and to their husbands. She loved them both. Their folks would find other husbands for them and they could have happy lives. She had nothing more to offer them.

Orpah kissed her mother-in-law and left for home. But Ruth knew that this old lady she loved would not be able to make that long trip alone. She would die on the way with no one to help her. So, Ruth told Naomi she was going to go with her.

Naomi tried to persuade her to go home, but Ruth said, "Don't ask me to leave you or to return from following after you; for wherever you go, I will go, and where you stay, I will stay, Your people will be my people, and your God, my God. Where you die, I will die, and there will I be buried."

With a vow like that, Naomi could do nothing to persuade her to leave, so she quit trying.

After a long, arduous journey, they came to Bethlehem, Naomi's former home. The ladies recognized Naomi and commiserated with her as she told them of her bad fortune and the loss of her men. Naomi felt that the Lord had treated her badly. She told them to call her Mara, which meant "bitter."

When they arrived in Bethlehem, it was at the beginning of barley harvest.

Naomi had told Ruth how the Lord provided for the poor and widows in Israel. They were allowed to go out and pick up what was left in the fields after the harvesters had been through. It was called gleaning. They needed food, so Ruth went out to glean.

She happened to get into the field of a man named Boaz. Boaz was a good, godly man. He was kind to all his workers. They respected him and loved him. He knew them all. When he looked out over his field, he saw this strange woman. He asked who she was. His overseer told him it was the Moabitess girl who had come back with Naomi. She had asked him for permission to glean in the field, and he had given it.

Boaz went to Ruth and told her to stay with his reaper girls through all their fields and drink from their water jars. He said that he had told the young men to leave her alone, and she would be safe in his fields.

Ruth was impressed with the kindness of Boaz. It was so unusual for anyone to treat a stranger that well. Boaz told her that he had heard what she had been doing for her mother-in-law, how she had come to this strange country and was taking care of Naomi. He asked God's blessing upon her.

Boaz told her to come and eat lunch with his people. He made sure she got plenty. Then Boaz told his men to let some of the grain fall to the ground so that she could pick it up and not to scold her for it. Ruth gleaned all day.

That night, Naomi was surprised at how much Ruth brought home. She asked where Ruth had gleaned. When Ruth told her, Naomi was pleased. She said that Boaz was a blessing. He was also one of their nearest relatives, called a kinsman.

She told Ruth, "Do as he says. Stay near his girls. Don't go into anyone else's fields." So, Ruth stayed in Boaz's fields all through the barley and wheat harvests. She lived with her mother-in-law and took care of her.

It seems that Boaz had never married, though he was a very wealthy man. Perhaps the men of the country had refused to give him their daughters because he was not a full blooded Israelite. His mother was Rahab, the former prostitute, who had helped the spies of Joshua when they went into Jericho. So Boaz knew what it was like to try to fit into a country, being a stranger. He had watched his mother trying to do that, so he had extra compassion for Ruth.

Naomi had noticed how well Ruth spoke of Boaz as she had watched and visited with him all summer, working in his fields.

Naomi decided it was time for her to do something to get Ruth a husband. She knew all the laws and rules of her nation. One of them was that it was the responsibility of the nearest kinsman to marry the widowed wife of his kinsman. She made a plan and told Ruth exactly how to carry it out.

Though Ruth didn't really understand all the implications, she obeyed her mother-in-law exactly, as she had been doing for years.

Ruth was to clean herself up and go down to the barley floor where Boaz was threshing, that night. She was not to let anyone see her. She was to wait until everything was done, Boaz had eaten, laid down to sleep, and was sound asleep. Then she was to go uncover his feet and lie down at his feet.

When he woke, he would tell Ruth what to do.

Ruth did all this exactly as Naomi had told her.

At midnight, when he turned over, Boaz realized he was not alone. He looked and there was a woman at his feet! He asked, "Who is there?"

She replied, "I am Ruth, your handmaid. Spread your garment over your handmaid, for you are a near kinsman" (words Naomi had instructed her to say to him).

Boaz commended her for being so kind. He said he had noticed she had not run after the young men around her, all summer long. Everyone knew that she was a virtuous woman. He would marry her if he could, but there was another man who was a closer kinsman that he.

Boaz loaded Ruth up with grain to take to Naomi and told her, "Hurry home before anyone sees you and draws wrong conclusions."

Naomi knew Boaz would settle things that day, so they waited.

Early in the morning, Boaz went to the city gate where business was done. When his kinsman came by, he stopped him. Then he stopped ten important men to be witnesses. He told the kinsman that Naomi was selling a parcel of land that was Elimelech's. Since he was the nearest kinsman, did he want to buy it?

The kinsman said, "Yes."

Then Boaz told him, "If you buy it, you must also take Ruth, the Moabitess, and raise up sons for her to carry on the name of her dead husband"---sons, who would inherit the land.

The kinsman changed his mind then, and said, "I cannot redeem it myself. It would hurt my own inheritance. Since you are next in line, you redeem it."

So, the kinsman took off his shoe and gave it to Boaz in front of all the witnesses, a sign that it was done. Of course, this was exactly what Boaz had planned.

He announced to everybody, "You are witnesses. Today I am buying everything that was Elimelech's, Chilion's and Mahlon's from Naomi, including Ruth, the Moabitess, so that the name of the dead will not be cut off."

So Boaz married Ruth. They had a son. They named him Obed. He became the father of Jesse, who became the father of King David and the ancestor of Jesus Christ.

Naomi lived with Ruth and Boaz and helped care for Obed. All the women said of her, "Blessed be the Lord, who has not left you without a kinsman. Here is little Obed, born of your daughter-in-law who loves you, and is better to you than seven sons."

Our next hero is Samuel, a child asked of God and given back to God, who accepted his God-given role and made the most of it. He led his nation for years and kept them serving God, all his lifetime.

Samuel

There was a man named Elkanah who had two wives. One was named Hannah; the other named Peninnah. Peninnah had children; Hannah had none.

Elkanah loved Hannah, but It was customary in those days to have as many wives as a man could take care of. He needed children to carry on his name and keep the family fortune together. So, if his wife couldn't produce children, he married another one who could. It was a great grief to Hannah to have no children, and Peninnah taunted her continually about it.

Every year, Elkanah took his family up to the house of the Lord at Shiloh to sacrifice and worship the Lord, there.

Eli, the priest, lived there. His two sons, Hophni and Phinehas, were priests there, helping him.

One year when they went to the house of the Lord, Hannah was especially burdened with her barrenness. She wept and prayed over it. She went before the Lord and prayed. She asked Him for a son. She promised that if God gave her a son, she would give him back to the Lord, all the days of his life. He would live as a Nazirite, never drink strong drink and never shave his head.

Her lips were moving as she silently prayed. Eli the priest saw her and thought she was drunk because she was in such agony. He scolded her. Hannah told him about her prayer for a son. Eli told her to go in peace, that God would answer her prayer. Hannah went away happy.

In the next year, Hannah had a son. She called the name of her son, Samuel, because she had asked God for him, and God had given him to her.

That year, Hannah did not go up to Shiloh. She said she would wait until Samuel was weaned. Then she would take him to the house of the Lord and leave him forever. Elkanah said for her to do whatever seemed right to her.

When Samuel was old enough, they went up to Shiloh, taking three bullocks, one ephah of flour and a bottle of wine as sacrifices to the Lord, and they took Samuel. They presented him to Eli and told him this was the son Hannah had prayed for. Now she was giving him to the Lord, as she had promised.

Samuel worshipped there. He seemed to be old enough to know what was going on. There were many children of the priests around. The child was left in the care of the priests. He served in the temple. He wore a little linen ephod. His mother and father went back home without him. Every year, his mother made him a little coat and brought it to him. Over the years, God gave her five more children.

Eli's sons were wicked. They did not serve God as the priests were supposed to. Instead, they were immoral. They demanded extra sacrifices for themselves and cheated the people, so that the people despised the sacrifices to the Lord. Eli warned his sons, but he did not stop them in their wicked ways. Samuel did not get involved with them.

A prophet came to Eli and scolded him for not stopping his sons from their wickedness. He said, "God says, 'Those who honor me, I will honor.'" He said that Eli's family would be cut off because of their sins.

Samuel was well liked by both God and people. He was a constant help to Eli. One night, as Samuel was lying in bed, he heard a voice calling his name, "Samuel, Samuel."

Samuel answered, "Here I am." He thought it was Eli wanting him for something, so he got up and ran into Eli's room and asked him what he wanted.

Eli told him, "I didn't call you. Go back to bed." This happened three times. It had been a long time since God had spoken to anybody, but, finally, Eli realized it was God calling the child, so he told him, "Go back to bed, and if the voice comes again, say, 'Speak, Lord, for your servant hears.'"

So, Samuel went back to his bed. The Lord came and stood at the foot of his bed and called his name, "Samuel, Samuel."

Samuel answered, "Speak, for your servant hears."

God told him He was going to judge Eli's family because of their sins.

Samuel was afraid to see Eli the next morning, but Eli found him and demanded that he tell him everything the Lord had said to him. Samuel told him every bit of it. Eli said, "It is the Lord; let Him do whatever seems good to Him."

The Lord was with Samuel as he grew and people listened to him. All Israel knew that Samuel was a chosen prophet of God.

The Ark of God

The Philistines went to war against Israel. Israel was losing the battle. The Israelites decided to take the Ark of the Covenant into battle with them, thinking that if the ark was there, God would fight for them and make them win. The two sons of Eli, Hophni and Phinehas, went along with the Ark.

The Philistines were worried about Israel's God! They had heard about all the times He had fought for Israel and wiped out their enemies. But they fought extra hard that day and defeated Israel. They killed Eli's two sons, and captured the Ark of God.

One of the Israelites escaped and ran to Shiloh, where Eli sat by the wayside waiting to hear about the battle and the Ark of God.

Eli was heavy, 98 years old and blind. They told him that the battle was lost and his sons were killed. But when they said, "And the Ark of God was taken," he fell backward, broke his neck and died.

Phinehas' wife was giving birth when she heard the terrible news. It was devastating to her, and she died, after having a son, whom she named "Ichabod," for she said, "The glory of the Lord is departed from Israel, for the Ark of God is taken."

After they had the Ark, the Philistines didn't know what to do with it, so they put it in the temple of Dagon, their god. The next morning, Dagon was on his face before the Ark. They set him back up.

The following morning, Dagon was not only on his face before the Ark, but his head and both palms of his hands were cut off and lying on the threshold. Only the stump of Dagon was left. The Philistines were upset and frightened.

Then the country was suddenly overrun with rats and they all began to have tumors on their private parts. This really scared them!

They couldn't wait to get rid of the Ark. They sent it to Gath.

Gath developed the same trouble; so they sent it on to Ekron. Ekron had the same results. People died or had tumors, and rats were everywhere.

The Ark of God was in the country of the Philistines for seven months.

Finally, the Philistines had had enough of it; so the leaders got together and tried to decide how to get rid of it. The heathen priests told them to send it back to Israel, but to send a trespass offering with it, so that God would remove His hand from them and they would be healed.

So, they put together a special offering of five golden tumors and five golden rats, because there were five lords of the Philistines.

They were to give glory to the God of Israel, take a new cart, put the jewels in a container on it, hook it up to two milk cows that had never had a yoke on them before, take their calves away from them, and set the Ark on the road toward Israel.

If the cart went to Israel, they would know that it really was the God of Israel who had done all these things to them. If it didn't, they would know it had all just been coincidence. They did exactly as the priests had said. The cows went straight down the road toward Israel, bawling all the way.

The Philistines followed to see if the cows would actually take it home. They did. The cart came into the field of a man named Joshua in Beth Shemesh and stopped there.

The men were threshing wheat. When they looked up and saw the Ark coming home they rejoiced. They broke up the cart and sacrificed the cattle to the Lord as a burnt offering.

The Philistines had been very careful to be respectful to the Ark of God, even though they worshipped Dagon.

The Israelites knew they were not to touch the Ark, but people looked into it, anyway, handled it wrongly, and were punished for it.

They sent it on to Kiriath Jearim. There it stayed for twenty years because they were afraid to bring it home. They seemed to have forgotten how to handle the Ark the way God had told them.

Samuel told the people they must get rid of their false gods and worship the Lord only. The people gathered at Mizpah to worship and reconsecrate themselves to God.

When the Philistines heard they were there, they came down to fight.

Samuel made an offering to God and prayed. God thundered against the Philistines and Israel won the battle.

Samuel took a stone and set it up between Mizpah and Shen, and called it Ebenezer, saying, "Thus far has the Lord helped us."

The Philistines gave back the cities they had taken and didn't bother Israel all the time Samuel was alive and judging Israel.

Saul had everything going for him. He was tall, good looking, brave, and loved God when he was chosen to be Israel's first king, but it all went to his head and he became too proud of himself and concerned about what the people thought, instead of what God thought and wanted from him.

He started out well, but ended up a failure. At times, he was a scoundrel. He is not a hero, though he could have been.

A King---Saul

Samuel was old. He set his sons up as judges, but his sons were not as he was; they were like Eli's sons had been. They took bribes and went after the money instead of God. The people were not happy with them. They went to Samuel and told him they wanted a king like the other nations around them had.

Samuel was not happy with their idea of a king. He went to God about it.

God told him that the people were not rejecting Samuel; they were rejecting God from ruling over them. God told Samuel to make them a king, but first to tell them what the results of having a king would be: The king would take their sons and daughters as servants, he would have them working for him, he would take taxes from them; but worst of all, they would be losing the Lord as their King.

The people still wanted a king so they could be like all the nations around them. Samuel sent them all away and said that he would anoint them a king.

Now there was a Benjamite named Kish, a mighty, powerful man. He had a son named Saul.

Saul was a very good man. He was physically strong. He was a head taller than any of the people.

Kish had some donkeys that ran away so he sent his son, Saul, to take a servant and go look for them. They looked and looked but couldn't find them. Finally, they were about to go home, but decided, since they were near the town of Samuel, to stop and ask him about the donkeys. They did.

When they got there, Samuel came out to meet them because the Lord had told him the day before that Saul was coming. He was to anoint Saul to be king of Israel.

Samuel invited Saul and his servant up to the feast he had arranged to be prepared for him. He gave him the special food he had set aside just for Saul. He told him that his father's donkeys had been found days ago. He also said that Saul was to be special to all Israel. He kept them there that night.

The next day, Samuel had the servant go on ahead. Then he told Saul that he was to be king. He anointed Saul with oil, kissed him, and told him exactly what was going to happen to him on the way home.

Samuel said, "Two men will meet you and tell you that your father's donkeys were found, and your father is worried about you. Then you will meet three men going up to worship, carrying three kids, three loaves of bread and a wine skin. They will salute you and give you two loaves of bread. You are to take the loaves."

"Then, as you go further, you will meet a group of prophets coming down from worship, playing musical instruments and prophesying. The Spirit of the Lord will come upon you with power, and you will prophesy and God will change your heart, and make you into a new person."

After Saul got home, he was to go to Gilgal to meet Samuel, who would make offerings to the Lord. He was to stay there seven days.

When Saul left Samuel, all these things happened to him, exactly as Samuel had said they would. God was with Saul in a mighty way.

When he got home, Saul didn't mention to anyone what Samuel had told him or that he had anointed him to be king.

When Samuel came to Mizpah, he reminded the people of all the things their God had done for them. Then he had all the tribes line up before the Lord. They drew lots, and the tribe of Benjamin was taken. They continued to draw lots down to Kish, where Saul's name was drawn.

They looked around for Saul and couldn't find him. Saul had hidden among the baggage. They ran and brought him out to all the people. When he stood with them, he was head and shoulders taller than anyone else. He had a kingly look about him.

Samuel introduced him to all the people and told them that this was the man that the Lord had chosen to be their king.

The people shouted, "God save the King!" Then Samuel wrote in a book what the kingdom was to be like, and sent all the people away.

Saul also went home to Gibeah, but a band of men, whose hearts God had touched, went with him.

Others said, "How can this man save us?" and hated him. But Saul didn't say a thing about them, or to them. He just took it with grace.

The Kingdom

The Ammonites encamped outside Jabesh Gilead to make war against them. They threatened to put out the right eye of every man, as a reproach against Israel. Jabesh sent word to Saul of what was happening. The Spirit of the Lord came upon Saul. He sent word to all Israel to come to him. They came. They utterly defeated the Ammonites there.

Saul and Samuel went to Gilgal where they all renewed the kingship, worshipped the Lord, and gave thanks to Him for saving them.

Samuel reminded them again of all the mighty works their God had done for them down through the years. He told them again, that if they and their king served the Lord, the Lord would bless them. If they didn't, the Lord would punish them.

After Saul had reigned for two years, he chose three thousand men of Israel. Two thousand were with Saul in Micmash and a thousand with his son, Jonathan, in Gibeah.

In Gibeah, Jonathan fought a garrison of the Philistines and won. All the Philistines were upset by this. They gathered thousands of chariots and a vast army to fight against Saul. It scared the men of Israel half to death!

Saul waited seven days for Samuel to come to him as he had said he would. Samuel wasn't there, yet, and Saul's army got scared and began to desert him. So, instead of waiting for Samuel, as Samuel had told him to do, Saul took it upon himself to make an offering to the Lord of a burnt sacrifice.

Just as he finished up, Samuel came. Samuel said, "What have you done? You have not obeyed the commandment of the Lord! If you had, God would have established your kingdom forever. But now, God has taken your kingdom away from you and will give it to another who will obey Him." Then Samuel left.

Saul counted his army. He was down to about six hundred men. In fear, Saul and his little army sat at the foot of the mountain and did nothing.

The Israelites didn't have swords or spears. They didn't have any way of working iron. They didn't know how. They had to get their swords from the Philistines. So, only Saul and his son, Jonathan, had swords.

Jonathan got tired of just sitting there waiting for the Philistines to do something. So, he told his armor bearer that they were going to climb up the mountain where the enemy encampment was and see if the Lord wouldn't use them to do something for His people.

He said, "God doesn't care how many are fighting on His side. He can use many or few!"

Meanwhile, Saul sat in the camp under a pomegranate tree with his men, doing nothing. Jonathan didn't tell his father his plans. He and his armor bearer just went.

When they were almost to the top, Jonathan told his armor bearer, "We will let them see us, and if they say 'Wait until we come to you,' we won't go on up to them. But if they say, 'Come up to us,' we will go up, because we will know the Lord has given us the victory over them."

The Philistines said, "Come up to us, and we will show you a thing."

So, Jonathan and his man went clawing their way to the top. They began to fight the Philistines. They killed about twenty men.

God sent an earthquake, and all the enemy began to fight each other and run away. The Philistine army seemed to just melt away.

Saul saw it from the bottom of the mountain. He asked who was missing of his army. He found out that Jonathan and his armor bearer were gone.

All the men who had been hiding came out and chased the Philistines. The army came, too, but most of the damage was done by the earthquake and the Philistines fighting each other. The Lord saved Israel that day, using Jonathan and his man.

Saul had called a fast that day, so no one ate anything all day.

They came to a wooded area and there was honey on the ground.

Jonathan had not heard about his father's foolish decree, so he ate some honey. He had been fighting a long time and he needed strength. The little honey he ate gave him strength.

Saul was about to have Jonathan killed for eating when he had declared a fast, but the people would not allow it. They said it was Jonathan who had saved Israel, with God's help, and he was not going to die for breaking Saul's rules. So, they saved him.

Saul fought all the battles of Israel against their enemies.

His sons were: Jonathan and Ishvi, Malki-Shua and Ish-Bosheth. His daughters were: Merab and Michal. The captain of his army was Abner, Saul's cousin.

There was war against the Philistines all the days of Saul. He took any strong or valiant man into his army.

Samuel told Saul that he was to fight against the Amalekites and utterly destroy them and everything they had. Saul took an army and did it. But he spared the king, Agag, and all the best of the cattle, sheep, and oxen.

When Saul didn't obey as God had commanded him, God told Samuel that He had rejected Saul as king of Israel because he didn't know how to obey his commands. Samuel felt so badly about it that he cried all night.

In the morning, he went to Saul at the battlefield.

Saul came up to him and said, "Blessed is the name of the Lord. I have done all He told me to do."

Samuel replied, "Then, what is all this mooing of cattle and bleating of sheep that I hear?"

Saul said:" The PEOPLE have done all this. They saved the best to sacrifice to the Lord, YOUR GOD. But we have destroyed all the rest."

Samuel told him, "When you were little in your own sight, God anointed you to be king of Israel, but now you think you are too big and important to obey the Lord."

When Saul kept blaming the people, Samuel told him. "To obey is better than sacrifice; and to listen is better than the choicest gifts." Then he told Saul that God had rejected him from being king, because "Rebellion is as bad as witchcraft, and stubbornness is like idolatry."

Saul admitted that he had sinned. He wasn't really sorry; only that he gotten caught at it.

When Samuel started to leave, Saul asked him to go before the people with him anyway, to make himself look good.

When Samuel refused, Saul grabbed his robe to force him to stay, but the robe tore.

Samuel told Saul, "God has torn the kingdom of Israel from you, today, and will give it to another, who will obey him."

Then Samuel went before the people with Saul to worship the Lord and give Saul prestige before the people, as he wanted.

Saul was always more interested in pleasing the people than in pleasing the Lord.

Samuel never went to see Saul again until he died. But Samuel grieved for Saul. God was unhappy that He had made Saul king.

Finally, God said to Samuel, "How long will you keep grieving over Saul because I have rejected him as king? Take your horn of oil and go to Bethlehem to a man named Jesse. I have chosen a king from among his sons."

Samuel knew that if Saul heard he'd anointed a king, he would kill Samuel. God told him to take an offering with him and tell them that he had come to make an offering to the Lord, there. He was to invite Jesse and his sons, and God would show him which of the sons He had chosen. Samuel was to anoint him, make his offering, then come back home.

When Samuel saw Jesse's sons, they were all tall and handsome. Samuel thought each one of them looked like he must be the one God had chosen.

God told him, "Man looks at the outside, but the Lord looks on the heart."

Finally, after seven sons had passed before him and God had said, "No, it's not that one, either," Samuel asked Jessie, "Is this all your sons?"

Jessie told him, "No, the youngest one is still out in the fields taking care of the sheep." (They hadn't thought he was worth inviting to the feast).

Samuel told him, "Send and get him, because we will not sit down to supper until he gets here."

When David came in, he was a handsome young man, too.

The Lord told Samuel, "Rise and anoint him, because he is the one I have chosen."

So Samuel anointed David in front of all his brothers.

Samuel went home. And the Spirit of the Lord came upon David from that day forward.

The Spirit of the Lord left Saul, and an evil spirit came upon him. Saul would fall into a bad state of depression, and anger would fill his heart and mind. His servants suggested that he needed music to cheer him up. So, they looked for a man who could play the harp well.

One of the servants suggested that Jesse's son, David, could play well, was a good fighter, and the Lord was with him. So David was sent for. He came and played for Saul when he was depressed. It cheered Saul up and Saul grew to love David.

David stayed with Saul and became his armor bearer. David stayed awhile; but Saul was so improved, that David went home.

David is a real hero. He started out the youngest in a big family of boys, not worth mentioning as far as the family was concerned, but God saw his heart. God knew that even when David made mistakes, even sinned, he was most concerned about what God thought of him. He always repented and asked for God's forgiveness. God could use a man like that, and He did.

We remember David's songs to the Lord, called Psalms. They speak of God's love, and our love for God. David had a caring, shepherd's heart.

David

The Philistines came to war against Israel, again. They settled on a mountain on one side, with the Israelites on the mountain on the other side and a valley in between the two armies.

The Philistines sent out a giant, nine feet tall. He had a monstrous spear, body armor and a man to carry his shield in front of him. He had a huge helmet on his head and armored leggings, so nothing much was exposed.

He shouted challenges to the army of Israel, "Send a man out. Come fight against me. If your man beats me, we will be your slaves. If I destroy your man, you will all be our slaves."

Israel had always been afraid of giants. The men of Israel were terrified of him. His name was Goliath. Every day, at a certain time, Goliath would come out and shout at the army of Israel, challenging them and cursing their God. For forty days Goliath did this, with Saul and the army of Israel sitting there, afraid to do anything about it.

Jesse's three oldest sons were in Saul's army. David had again been given the job of shepherd when he got home. He was just "the kid."

One day, Jesse sent for him and told him he was to take food to his brothers and to their superior officers at the army camp, find out how his brothers were getting along and about the battle. So David left the sheep with a keeper and went.

He got to the army camp. While he was talking with his brothers, the giant, Goliath, came out as before. When David heard it, he was shocked. David saw immediately that this was an insult to God, while his brothers and the army saw it as a threat to themselves. He asked, "What is being done about this giant who dares to defy the Living God?"

His brothers were angry with him that he even asked such a question; but others standing by heard him and went and told Saul that there was a man in the camp who was willing to go and fight against Goliath.

Saul called for David to come to him. When he saw him, Saul said, "You can't go and fight against this giant. You are just a kid! He is a man of war from his youth!"

David assured Saul, "I killed a lion and a bear, while taking care of my father's sheep. God will give me this heathen giant, who dares to call down curses on Him."

Saul said to at least take his armor, but when David put it on, he could hardly move in it, it was so big for him. David took off the armor.

He told Saul, "I will go in the strength of the Lord."

David took his sling. He chose five smooth stones from the river bed and put them in his shepherd's bag. (Goliath had four brothers almost as big as he was). David was prepared. He took his sling in his hand and started out for Goliath.

Goliath saw this kid coming. He began to taunt him and his God. He told him what he was going to do to him.

David said to Goliath, "You come to me with a sword, a shield, and a spear, but I come to you in the name of the Lord of Hosts, the God of the armies of Israel, whom you have defied. I will take your head off, and all the earth will know that there is a God in heaven. The battle is the Lord's!"

Then David pulled out one of the stones, put it in his sling and hurled it toward the giant. He only needed one, though he still had four more, in case the giant's brothers joined in the fight.

The stone hit Goliath in the middle of the forehead, almost the only place that wasn't covered with armor. Goliath fell to the ground like a huge tree. David ran to him, picked up Goliath's sword and cut the giant's head off with it.

When the Philistines saw their champion dead, they all ran away as fast as they could. The army of Saul finally woke up and chased after them, completely routing the enemy.

David was Jonathan's kind of man. Jonathan and David became fast friends. Jonathan gave David his sword, his bow; even his robe. He loved David.

David went back with Saul's army. Saul put him in charge of the men of war. Everybody loved David and accepted him.

As was the custom, the women came out, singing, as the men were returning from the battle. They sang: "Saul has killed his thousands; and David his ten thousands."

Saul heard this. It made him furious to be put second. He said, "What can David have more but the kingdom?"

The next day, the evil spirit came upon Saul while David was playing his harp for him. There was a javelin in Saul's hand. He threw the javelin at David, planning to kill him. But David dodged at just the right time and escaped.

Saul was afraid of David because the Lord was with David and had left Saul. Saul, hoping he would get killed, made David captain over a thousand men, so that he had to go with the people to battle. David behaved himself wisely, and all the people loved him. This made Saul even more afraid of him.

Trouble

Saul had promised that anyone who killed Goliath would get to marry his oldest daughter; but David was hesitant about becoming the king's son-in-law, and Saul married her off to another man, instead.

Then he found out that his youngest daughter, Michal, loved David. He thought to use her to get rid of David. He told David that if he brought proof to him that he had killed one hundred Philistines, he could marry Michal. Saul's plan was that David would end up being killed by the Philistines, and Saul would be rid of him.

David thought it was such a great honor to marry the king's daughter that he brought proof he had killed two hundred.

Saul was disappointed, but he gave Michal to David and they were married. Now that he was the king's son-in-law, Saul became even more afraid of David.

Saul tried to convince Jonathan and all his servants that they should kill David. Nobody agreed with him, especially his son, Jonathan, who loved David.

Jonathan took his father out into the field, talked to him, and reminded him of all the good things David had done for him and the kingdom. He convinced Saul that David would never do anything against him; so Saul said that he would quit trying to kill David.

Then there was war again and David won many battles. The evil spirit came upon Saul again and he determined to kill David. He threw a spear at him, but David avoided it.

Saul sent to his house and ordered David to be brought to him; but Michal heard of his plot, so Michal let David down through a window and he ran away.

Michal put an idol and some goat's hair in his bed to make it look like he was there. When the messengers came for David, she told them he was sick. Saul sent others, telling them to bring David to him in his bed!

When he found out that David was gone, he was angry with Michal for deceiving him. She lied and said that she had helped him because David had threatened to kill her if she didn't help him escape.

David went to Samuel and stayed. Everyone who came to capture him began to prophesy, even Saul, so David was safe for awhile, but he wanted to go home. He went back to see Jonathan to ask him what he should do. He knew he could trust Jonathan. He was his friend.

They set up a plan so that David could know if it was safe to come home. David was to hide in the field and see what Saul would say if he were not at dinner for three days. If Saul was angry, Jonathan would let David know that it was not safe to come home. Jonathan would come out into the field with a boy and shoot arrows. Jonathan said, "If I tell the lad, 'The arrows are on this side', it means that it is safe to come home. If I say to the boy, 'The arrows are beyond you,' that means it is not safe to come home and you must run away, because Saul is still trying to kill you."

At dinner the second day, Saul was furious about David not being there. He even threw a spear at Jonathan because he knew that Jonathan loved David and was trying to help him. He told Jonathan, "You will never get to be king as long as David lives".

Jonathan did as he had told David he would do. He warned him with the arrows. Then he sent the boy back home and waited for David to come out. They cried together and pledged faithfulness to each other and protection for their families from each other--whoever became king. Then David left and Jonathan went into the city. He was still his father's son and heir to the throne.

David went to the priest of Nob, got hallowed bread from him which was only for the priests, and the sword of Goliath, which was stored there, because he didn't have any weapon with him.

Then he went to Gath, a Philistine city, whose king's name was Achish. When someone reminded Achish that the people had sung, "David has killed his ten thousands," David knew he was in great trouble, so he pretended to be crazy. He knew people were afraid of a crazy man.

Achish was not interested in having a crazy man there. He let him go.

So, David escaped to the cave of Adullam.

When his brothers and family heard of it, they went to him, there. It was not safe for anybody who liked or was related to David.

Everyone who was in trouble with Saul, or in debt, or unhappy about things, went and stayed with David, until he had about four hundred men with him all the time, an army of misfits.

David took his parents to Moab to stay, so they would be safe.

Saul found out that the priests of Nob had helped David, even though they told him they knew nothing about Saul's enmity against him. A spy had told Saul about their helping David. Since nobody else would, Saul had the spy kill the priests. He killed about eighty-five priests, all the people in that place who had helped David. David felt terrible that he had been the cause of their deaths. When one of them, Abiathar, escaped and came to him, he kept him with him to be their priest.

In Hiding

David was in hiding from Saul. He did nothing without asking the Lord if he should do it. God directed him in everything, and David listened and obeyed. He fought battles rescuing cities from the Philistines, but leaving before they could turn him over to Saul. Everyone was in danger if Saul learned that they had helped David.

Jonathan came to David in secret at one time to encourage him. They repeated their pact to look after each other and their families. Jonathan told David that he knew David would be king some day and he would be his helper, and that was good. He always was a great encourager to David, and a faithful friend. Jonathan was a hero.

Saul fought other battles, but whenever the battle was over, he again chased David, trying to kill him, so that David could never take over his position as king or replace Jonathan for the throne.

One day, as Saul was chasing David with 3,000 men, Saul went into a cave by himself. He didn't know that David and some of his men were deep in the cave.

While he was in there, David and his men crept up on him. David's men encouraged him to kill Saul. David cut off a little piece of Saul's robe. Then he even felt sorry about that, for he said, "Saul is the Lord's anointed, and I won't touch him to hurt him."

When Saul left the cave, David came out, bowed to the ground before him and told him what he had done and showed him the scrap from his robe. He said, "You have never had a reason to be afraid of me. I have never been Saul's enemy."

Saul realized that David could have killed him, but didn't. Saul said he knew that one day David would be king, and he pledged him to be good to Saul's family when he became king. Then Saul went home. But David and his men went far away, again. David knew he couldn't trust Saul.

Then the prophet, Samuel, died. All Israel lamented his passing.

David and his men had been in the area of Carmel for a long time. They had protected the sheep and property of a very rich man named Nabal.

When David heard that Nabal was shearing sheep, he sent some of his young men to Nabal to ask him for food for his men. He knew there would be a great feast for Nabal's shearers, and they wouldn't even miss the extra food.

Nabal answered the men in a surly manner, telling them, "I don't know David, and I don't care about his men or his need. Don't bother me!"

David was so furious when he heard Nabal's attitude, after all he had done to protect him, that he had his men arm themselves and start out for Nabal's place to wipe him out.

One of Nabal's servants went to Nabal's wife, Abigail, and told her what was happening, and how rude Nabal had been to David's men, who had been so good to all of them and helped them so much.

Abigail knew what a stinker her husband was, so she took two hundred loaves of bread, two skins of wine, five dressed sheep, five measures of grain, a hundred cakes of raisins and two hundred fig cakes. She put them on donkeys and started out for David's camp, herself. She didn't tell any of this to her husband.

Abigail met David as he and his men were coming, intent on killing every man in Nabal's camp. She told him that she hadn't known about the young men he had sent, but to please forgive them for being so cold to them. She had brought a peace offering to him. She praised God that he had not killed anyone yet, because, "When you become king, I don't want you to be sorry, or feel guilty for having shed innocent blood."

David was so impressed with Abigail, her attitude, and her advice, he praised the Lord for sending her and sent her home in peace, telling her that she had saved all her people.

When Abigail got home, Nabal was feasting with all his men. He was drunk. She waited until the next day to tell him what a close call he'd had. When he heard it, he had a stroke and died about ten days later.

Some time later, David sent for Abigail and asked her to be his wife. She went and lived with him at the camp. David also had a wife named Ahinoam. Saul had given David's wife, Michal, to a man named Paltiel.

More Treachery

Saul was again on the hunt for David. He took 3,000 men and his captain of the guard, Abner. They camped by the wilderness where David and his men were hiding.

David sent spies to find out exactly where they were. That night, David and his friend, Abishai, crept into Saul's camp while all were sleeping. Saul slept in the middle of the camp with his army all around him. David and Abishai crept up to him. Abishai wanted to kill Saul as he slept before them, but David said no, he would never hurt Saul because he was God's anointed. But they took his spear that was stuck in the ground beside Saul, and his water jug. Then they crept out of camp. Not a man woke up.

The next morning, David stood on the hill opposite Saul's camp and shouted at them. He scolded Abner for not protecting his master and showed them Saul's spear and water jug.

David asked Saul, "Who keeps telling you that David is your enemy?" He said Saul should know that it was a lie, because David had another opportunity to kill Saul, but he didn't, and wouldn't. David had somebody come over and get Saul's stuff. Saul repented again and went home with his soldiers.

David thought that he would one day be killed by Saul. He knew Saul wouldn't quit until he had killed him, or thought he was dead. He didn't ask God about it. Instead, he used his own wisdom and trusted himself---and panicked. David decided to go over into the camp of the Philistines.

He went to Achish, the king of Gath. He took his six hundred men and his two wives with him. It seemed to work for awhile, because when Saul heard that David was with the Philistines, he quit looking for him.

David asked Achish for a town to live in. Achish gave him Ziklag. David kept killing Philistines while he was in Ziklag, but he didn't leave anybody alive to tell about it. He let Achish think that he was raiding his own Israelite countrymen; so, Achish thought that David could never return home and would be his servant, forever.

David and his men stayed with the Philistines for a year and four months. God even brought good out of that, in spite of David's going on his own without asking God. While they were there, they learned how to work with iron. The Israelites had not known how, before. They had to get their spears and swords from the Philistines.

Then, Achish and the other Philistine leaders decided to go to war against Israel.

Saul had removed all the witches and wizards from the land; but when he saw all the Philistines coming to war against him, he was scared. He tried to pray, but God didn't answer him because Saul had turned against God, long ago. Saul thought he needed to hear from someone how to handle the coming battle. He asked his servant where there was a person who could call up the dead. The servant told him there was a witch at Endor.

Saul disguised himself and went to Endor at night. The woman was afraid when Saul asked her to bring up someone from the dead, knowing that Saul had had all of the witches killed. Saul promised her that nothing bad would happen to her, so she called up Samuel for him.

When the woman saw Samuel, she recognized Saul. She was terrified, but she told Saul what she had seen and what Samuel had said. The ghost of Samuel told Saul, "The Philistines will win the battle tomorrow. You and your sons will be killed. Israel will be defeated, and David will get the kingdom, just as God said."

Saul fell into a faint. The witch fed him and his men and they went home.

David and his men planned to go to battle along with the Philistines, but the other princes of the Philistines didn't trust him, so Achish sent him home.

When they got back to their town, they found that the Amalekites had come while they were gone, captured it, taken all their stuff, all their women and children and burned the city. David and his men were devastated. He finally inquired of the Lord. (It is the first time since David came to Achish that he has). He asked God if he should chase after the Amalekites.

God told him, "Yes, and you will get all of your people back."

So, David and his men went after them. Some of the men were too tired to go on, but those who did recovered every person, all the belongings and all the livestock.

When they got back to the men who were too worn out to go with them but had stayed with their stuff, some didn't want to share their gains, but David decreed that those who had stayed by the stuff would get equal shares with those who went into battle. It became a law, from then on.

David sent gifts of the plunder to all the cities of Israel where he and his men had hidden out.

Death of Saul

The Philistines were mighty in battle that day. They killed all three of Saul's sons, Jonathan, Abinadab, and Melch-ishua, and many other mighty men of Israel. The Philistines were winning. Saul was wounded badly, shot by an arrow. Saul told his armour bearer to kill him with his sword so that the Philistines wouldn't get him. but his armourerbearer would not do it, so Saul set the sword up in such a way that when he fell on it, he died. When his armourerbearer saw what Saul had done, he killed himself, too.

When the people of the towns around heard that Saul and his sons were all dead, they fled from the cities and ran for their lives. The Philistines came in and lived in the cities.

The Philistines found the bodies of Saul and his sons, stripped them of their finery, cut off Saul's head and proclaimed victory throughout their land in the temples of their idols. They fastened the bodies of Saul and his sons to the wall of a city, for everybody to see and scoff at.

When the men of Jabesh Gilead, remembering how Saul had saved them years ago, heard of it, they went at night and stole the bodies and brought them back, burned them and buried them under a tree at Jabesh and fasted seven days.

Now, when David got back from rescuing his people, an Amalekite came to his camp with a story of how the Israelites had been defeated. He told David that he was the one who had come upon Saul, wounded. Saul had asked him to kill him, so he did.

He told him that all Saul's sons were dead; Jonathan, too. He brought Saul's crown and bracelet to David, thinking he would get a huge reward. David asked him why he was not afraid to kill the Lord's anointed. Then David had him killed. The entire camp of David mourned and wept for Jonathan and Saul and Israel's army. David mourned greatly for Jonathan. He said his love for him was so very great.

David asked the Lord if he should go to any of the cities of Judah.

God told him to go to Hebron; so, he went with all of his men and his wives, and their wives, and lived in Hebron. The men of Judah came there and anointed David to be king.

When David heard what the men of Jabesh did by bringing back the bodies of Saul and his sons, he commended them for their bravery and goodness. He told them that he had been anointed king.

But Abner, Saul's army captain, anointed Ish-Bosheth, a son of Saul, to be king over the rest of Israel.

All the other tribes of Israel followed Ish-Bosheth, except the tribe of Judah, who followed David. For seven and a half years this went on.

One day, David's general, Joab, and Ish-Bosheth's general, Abner, were all together at a well in Gibeon. They each had their men with them. Abner suggested they have their young men fight for entertainment. They got up and fought with each other, killing each other. David's men won.

One of Joab's brothers was a very fast runner, and when Abner ran away from the battle, Asahel followed him. He ran so fast that Abner couldn't get away from him, but he knew who he was, so he called to him to stop chasing him. He didn't want to hurt Joab's brother.

Asahel didn't listen to him, but kept after him. When Asahel caught up to him, Abner killed him with his spear. The two armies decided to quit killing each other, since all of them were Israelites.

There was a long war between the followers of David and the followers of Saul's house. David continued to live in Hebron. His wives bore him sons: Amnon, Kileab, and Absalom, Adonijah, Shephatiah, and Ithream.

Abner was Ish-Bosheth's general, but he had a falling out with Ish-Bosheth over a woman. He had had enough of Ish-Bosheth, so he sent to David and told him that he would give him the kingdom if he would make an agreement with him.

David told him that he would see him, but he had to bring David's wife, Michal, with him. Abner did.

David made a great feast for Abner and his twenty men, and they made an agreement that all of Israel would be David's. Abner was sent away in peace, but Joab heard that he was going home, and he chased after him and killed him because he had killed his brother.

David was horrified. He had not had any part in this murder and told the people so. He wept over Abner, whom he said was a great soldier. The people were with David.

David Made King

Two of Ish-Bosheth's servants went in and killed him in his bed. Thinking that David would reward them, they took his head to David. David had them both killed, for being wicked men who would kill a righteous person in his bed, especially a king.

Then all the tribes came together and asked David to be their king. They remembered how David had helped Saul long ago and they wanted him to rule over them. So, the kingdom was reunited. David was 30 years old. He reigned for 40 years.

Hiram, King of Tyre, was a friend of David's. He sent cedar trees and carpenters and masons to build a house for David.

The Philistines went to war against David, but he defeated them. They came back again, and David asked the Lord how he should go to battle with them. God told him to get behind them where there were mulberry trees. When he heard the rustling in the tops of the mulberry trees, he was to go out and fight, because the Lord was fighting for him. God won the battle for him.

David went down to Gibeah where the Ark of the Lord was. He took a new cart and brought the Ark to Jerusalem. He made sacrifices. He put on a linen ephod and danced before the Lord. The people were so happy to have the Ark of God with them again, they shouted with gladness as David danced. He gave everyone special food and sent them all home.

After they had placed the Ark in its special place, David went home to Michal. Michal scolded and made fun of him for dancing in front of all the people, especially the women who saw him. David was very unhappy with her. He told her, "I was dancing before the

Lord, who chose me over your father to be King. And I will always honor the Lord, whether you approve of it or not."

Michal looked down her nose at him. David pretty much stayed away from her from then on. Michal never had any children.

A long time afterward, as David sat in his house, he told his friend, Nathan the prophet, that he wanted to build a house of worship for the Lord.

Nathan said, "That sounds like a wonderful idea. Go ahead and do it."

But that night God spoke to Nathan and told him, "The Lord doesn't live in houses. I am pleased that David wants to build me a house, but David is a man of war. He can't build my house, but his son will. Instead, I will build David's house and establish his name forever."

God said that after David died, GOD WAS GOING TO RAISE UP ONE OF HIS DESCENDANTS WHO WOULD ESTABLISH HIS KINGDOM FOREVER. David worshipped the Lord there.

David fought all the enemies of his country and beat all of them. He enlarged his territory, and his name was mighty in all the lands around him.

David looked to see if there were any of Jonathan's family left. He found out that Jonathan had a son, named Mephibosheth, still living. He had been a child when his father had been killed. His nurse had been running away to safety with him. She had tripped and fallen with him and injured him, so Mephibosheth was lame in both his feet.

David told him that, for his father's sake, he was to eat at the King's table as one of his sons; be cared for by Saul's old servant, Ziba and his sons; have the land that was his grandfather, Saul's; and Ziba was to farm it for him.

David fought many battles and won them all. But one time, at the time when they were to go to battle, he stayed behind and didn't go. He was bored one night with nothing to do, so he went up onto the house top of his palace. From there, he could look down on the city.

As he looked down, he could see on the house top of a nearby house a lady taking a bath. She was a beautiful woman. David stood and watched her.

He asked who she was. He was told she was Bathsheba, the granddaughter of one of his most trusted advisors, Ahithophel; the daughter of one of his best soldiers, Eliam; and the wife of one of his most loyal soldiers, Uriah the Hittite; all away doing battle for him.

There were red flags all over, because when one messed with a woman at that time, it was her men folk who were insulted.

David knew what God thought about that sort of thing, but he ignored all the warning signs. David had her brought to the palace.

She came to him and he had sex with her. Then he sent her home. It was sheer lust.

Bathsheba became pregnant, and she sent word to David, to tell him.

Uriah had not been home for many months, so it was obvious that he was not the father. To try to cover up his sin, David sent for Uriah to come home from the battle. He came.

David sent him home to be with his wife. But Uriah was too honorable. He didn't go home. He said that his king's army slept in the fields, and he would feel disloyal to go home and enjoy his wife's company.

So, in order to squirm out of the situation, David wrote a letter to his captain, Joab, telling him to put Uriah in the front of the battle, then move the troops back and let Uriah be killed. Joab did as David had directed him to do; and Uriah was killed.

David had many wives, but when her time of mourning was over, David, out of guilt, took Bathsheba as another of his wives.

Guilt

David thought nobody knew what he had done. But God knew. He sent Nathan, the prophet, to David, to confront him with his sins.

It was a dangerous assignment because kings in those days could have anybody killed they wanted to.

When he came to David, Nathan told him a story. He said, "Two men lived in a city. One was very rich. The other was so poor that he only had one little ewe lamb that he had raised and loved like a daughter."

"The rich man had many flocks of sheep, but when a traveler came to the rich man's house, he wouldn't get one of his many sheep to butcher and feed the man; instead, he took the poor man's one little lamb and killed it to feed his guest."

David, the former shepherd boy, was very angry. He declared, "The man who did this deserves to die! He should restore the lamb fourfold, because he had no pity."

Then Nathan pointed his finger at David and said, "You are the man! God said to tell you, 'I gave you your master's house, his wives, the house of Israel, and if you had needed any more, I would have given it to you. Why did you despise my commands and kill Uriah the Hittite, and take his wife for your own? Now, the sword will never leave your house. I will raise up evil in your own house.'"

David said, "I have sinned against the Lord." (He didn't make excuses or blame anybody else, and he realized that all sin is against God.)

Nathan told him that he would not die; but because of his wickedness, he had given people reason to doubt the Lord. David would be punished and the child would die.

The child got very sick. David prayed and fasted for him, hoping that God would change his mind, but God didn't and the child died.

David's servants were afraid to tell him, because he had been so sick with worry when the boy was sick. But when David realized that the child had died, he got up, washed his face and ate something.

His servants asked him why he did it that way.

David told them that he had hoped God would have mercy on him and let the child live. But now that the child was dead, he said. "I can't bring him back. I will go to him, but he won't come back to me." (He knew a baby was safe with God).

Then, David worshipped the Lord. His prayer is printed in the Bible, in Psalm 51, when he cried out for God to forgive him and renew a right spirit within him. He said his bones hurt while he was running from God in his sin.

Because David really was sorry for his sin against God and people, God forgave him. God said that David was "a man after His own heart."

Of course, David's family knew about David's sins, to a point. It shattered their ideas of their godly father. It opened the door for them to behave in their own lustful ways.

David had many sons and daughters. The oldest son was named Amnon. He was heir to the throne, as oldest son.

Amnon thought he was in love with his half sister, Tamar. Tamar had a brother, Absalom, who was very close to her. Tamar was a pure young princess and Amnon couldn't get close to her to do anything to her.

His cousin, Jonadab, knew of his infatuation with Tamar and his lust for her. He was a wicked, crafty man. He laid out a plan for Amnon to be able to rape his sister.

Amnon carried it out. Afterward, he hated her more than he had loved her. He pushed her out of his room and out of his house. He wouldn't listen to anything she said. Tamar tore her beautiful robe, put ashes on her head, and went out crying.

Her brother, Absalom, saw her and found out what had happened. He took her home to his house and told her not to say anything. To try to forget it. He never said a thing to his brother, Amnon, but he hated him for what he had done to his lovely sister.

When David heard of it, he was very angry, but he didn't do anything about it. He didn't punish Amnon. (He probably was thinking about his own sins).

About two years later, Absalom had a threshing party and invited all the king's sons. They all came; but his whole purpose was to kill Amnon, which he did. Absalom ran away. He stayed away for three years. David felt really bad about him and wanted him home, but he didn't do anything about it. David was a godly man, but he didn't seem to know how to discipline his sons, or how to show them love or forgiveness.

Absalom was a handsome, crafty man who thought he had been wronged by his father for not punishing his brother, Amnon. Absalom was a very proud man. He demanded his "rights" and set about to get them. He had no respect for his father or for his father's God. He is more a scoundrel than a hero.

Absalom

Now Joab, captain of the king's army, realized that David was sorry that Absalom stayed away as he did. David wanted him home, so Joab worked out a plan to get David to ask his son to come home.

Absalom came home, but David wouldn't see him or let him know that he was welcome. David couldn't seem to remember how God had so lovingly forgiven him for his own sins. David loved his son, but he couldn't seem to talk to him, or forgive him. David was a good man, but he was not a very good father to any of his children.

Absalom was there for two years, and he still had not seen his father.

Absalom sent for Joab, to get him to go to David and arrange for a meeting between him and his father. Joab didn't come, even after two times of asking him, so Absalom had his servants set fire to Joab's field, which was next to his own. Joab came. Then he went to David and got an audience with the king for Absalom. David kissed Absalom and welcomed him back. But Absalom had had all those years to nurse his anger and his feelings of resentment.

Absalom was an extremely handsome man, with long, thick hair and a handsome face. All the people admired him. Absalom prepared chariots and horses and fifty men to run before him as he moved about the city. He wanted an audience.

He would go and stand beside the city gate, and when any man would come to see the king for judgment, he would stop him, listen to him and tell him, "Nobody else will hear your case, but if I were king everybody would get a fair hearing." He implied that his father didn't have time for the people. He kept this up for a long time until he won over most of the people. They began to turn to him instead of King David.

After some years, Absalom went to Hebron, supposedly to make sacrifice to the Lord, but actually to make himself king. He even called David's chief counselor, Ahithophel, to go with him.

When David heard what was happening, he and all his court and all the people who were with him fled the city and went into the wilderness.

All the Levites came, too, bringing the Ark of the Covenant with them. But David sent the priests back with the Ark, saying, "If God wants me back, I will be back; but if not, whatever God wants is the way it should be." Then he prayed, "God, make Ahithophel's counsel come to nothing."

All the people went out, weeping. They loved King David.

One of his advisors, Hushai, wanted to go with David; but David sent him back to infiltrate Absalom's court and give him bad advice. Hushai went.

Absalom came into Jerusalem.

Ahithophel gave wonderful counsel to Absalom, and it looked like he would depose his father. Ahithophel told Absalom to go after his father and bring back all the people right away, because they were all weary from traveling; to kill the king only; then he could be king.

But Hushai gave different advice. He told him to wait; to remember that his father was a mighty man of battle and he would not stay with the people. He would be hidden somewhere, and in finding him people would die. Then they would turn against Absalom. He should get all the people with him before he did anything about following David.

Absalom listened to Hushai.

Hushai sent word to David to get on over the river with all his people. He told him what was happening in Jerusalem.

David divided his people into three groups, giving Joab one group, Abishai one, and Ittai one. David wanted to go with them, but the people told him he must stay in the city and be safe because he was the only important one.

As they left, David told his captains, "Deal gently, for my sake, with the young man, Absalom," and all the people heard it.

There was a great battle and many men were killed that day. They were fighting in a woods. As Absalom was riding his mule through the woods, his mule went under the thick boughs of an oak tree. His head, with the long, thick hair, got caught in the branches. His mule went on without him and left him hanging helplessly in the tree, caught by the head.

One of Joab's men saw Absalom and told him about it. The man who first saw him would not kill the king's son for any amount of money, but Joab was not so inclined. He found Absalom and killed him. They buried him in a big pit and piled a large heap of stones over his body.

When David was told, he was heartbroken. He wept for his son: "Oh Absalom, my son! My son, Absalom! Would God I had died for you! Oh, Absalom, my son, my son!"

Joab came to him and told him that he had shamed all the people who had stood by him. He said, "You love your enemies and hate your friends! Now go out and repair the damage you have done, or I will leave. And so will everyone else."

So, David went out and met with all the people and thanked them for going with him and winning the battle. Soon, the rest of Israel went out and called David back to his throne.

David was getting old.

David's son, Adonijah, was good-looking like his half brother Absalom had been, and he had the same ambition. He was next in line in age. David did nothing about his successor. Adonijah was thinking it was time he got the throne. He got chariots, horsemen and fifty men to run before him.

David didn't say a thing about it to him. Adonijah went to Joab the commander and Abiathar the priest, and they helped him. He called all of them, and the king's other sons, to come to a feast, but he didn't invite Zadok the priest, Benaiah, Nathan the prophet, or his brother, Solomon. He did all this to have himself declared king.

Nathan went to Bathsheba, David's wife, and told her she must go to David and ask him, "'Didn't you promise that my son, Solomon, would reign after you? Why then, is Adonijah reigning? You know that after you die, Solomon and I will be put to death by Adonijah if he is king.' And while you are still talking with him, I will come in and confirm it."

So, Bathsheba went to King David and told him what Nathan had said to tell him. Then, Nathan came in and told the king exactly what was happening.

David roused himself and set in motion all that needed to be done to declare Solomon king in his stead.

Solomon was anointed, put on David's mule and paraded through the towns, with trumpets blowing, and all the people shouting, "God save the King." David bowed to him and declared him King.

Solomon had a good start. He asked God for wisdom. God gave him not only wisdom, but riches beyond measure, unbelievable power and everything a man or a king could ask for. But in his old age, Solomon turned to the gods of his many wives and worshipped them instead of the God who had given him everything. In his last book, Ecclesiastes, he talks of the vanity of all things. One can only hope that he returned to his God in time. For many years, Solomon was a hero, but not a very dependable one.

Solomon

When the guests of Adonijah heard the noise of people shouting for Solomon and found out what it was, they all ran home as fast as they could. They tried to pretend that they had not been involved in crowning Adonijah king.

Adonijah feared for his life and ran and took refuge in the temple. Solomon told him he would live if he would behave.

Adonijah wasn't through; he went to Solomon's mother, Bathsheba, and asked her to go to King Solomon and ask him to let Adonijah marry Abishag, David's concubine. He thought that Solomon would not say no to his mother.

Solomon couldn't believe that his own mother was so foolish. He told her, "How foolish you are to ask such a thing! He might just as well ask for the throne!" He had Adonijah put to death that day.

David had told Solomon all the things he must do to establish his kingdom, whom to get rid of and whom to trust. Solomon listened well to his father and did what he told him to do.

Solomon went to Gibeon to sacrifice to the Lord. He built an altar and sacrificed a thousand burnt offerings there.

That night, Solomon had a dream. In the dream, God told him he could have anything he wanted. All he had to do was ask for it. Solomon told Him that he wanted wisdom to lead God's people. He wanted an understanding heart.

God was pleased and told him He would give him wisdom, but also all the things he had not asked for--wealth, power, honor, and long life, if he would walk in God's ways as his father David had.

Then Solomon woke up and it was a dream. But God did all the things He had promised in the dream.

One of the first cases to come to Solomon was this: Two prostitutes came with one baby. Both of them claimed the child was theirs. They had each had a child; but one of them had rolled on it in the night and smothered it. There seemed no way to tell which of the women was lying.

Solomon called for a sword and said, "Cut the baby in half and give half to each woman."

The baby's mother cried out, "No! Give the baby to her, but don't kill it!"

So Solomon knew the one who cared was really the mother, and gave the child to her. People were astonished at his wisdom.

Solomon made an agreement with the king of Egypt and married his daughter. It was an easy way to keep peace, so he repeated it over and over again, until he had 700 wives and 300 concubines.

David had gotten together much gold, silver, cedar wood, stone and all that would be needed to build a temple for the Lord. He made the plans, and Solomon was to carry them out. It was to be a magnificent house for God where the Ark would rest.

So, when he became king, much was already in place to help Solomon build God's house. Solomon went to King Hiram of Tyre, who was David's good friend. He told him that he was going to build the temple for God his father hadn't been allowed to build because he was a man of war. Hiram provided the rest of the cedar and pine trees for Solomon to build. Solomon sent food to Hiram for his nation. They became good friends.

Solomon laid the foundation of the temple to the Lord in the fourth year of his reign. It was a huge temple, made of costly stones and cedar. All the stones and lumber were precut so there was no pounding or cutting as they were building the temple. The whole temple was overlaid with gold, inside and out. It took seven years to build it. It was one of the wonders of the world at that time.

Solomon was a builder. He laid heavy taxes on the people to pay for all the building. It took thirteen years to build his own palace. He brought in a master craftsman to make all the brass candlesticks and other things that went into the temple and into his own house.

When the temple was all done they brought the Ark of the Covenant into it and put it in its special place. All the people came together to dedicate the temple. Solomon prayed a special prayer to the Lord asking his blessing on this temple and on this people. God's presence came down in such a heavy cloud it covered the temple. The priests could not even enter because of the Glory of the Lord that rested upon it.

Solomon offered to the Lord twenty-two thousand cattle and one hundred twenty thousand sheep as they dedicated the temple. Solomon had a great feast for fourteen days. He sent all the people home with food and joyful hearts.

After all the building was done, God came to Solomon again and told him that if he would continue to serve him as David had, He would establish his kingdom for as long as his sons and their sons served him. But if he turned aside, God's presence would not remain in the temple and He would turn against the people.

King Solomon built a navy, which no one in Israel had ever thought of doing. He worked with Hiram. They built on the shores of the Red Sea.

Hiram's men knew about sailing and helped Solomon. They sailed to Ophir and brought back great quantities of gold to King Solomon.

The queen of Sheba heard about Solomon, his wealth, his wisdom and his God. She came to see for herself if it was all true. She came in a camel caravan with lots of gold, spices, and precious stones. She was very impressed! She told Solomon that they hadn't told her half of how mighty he was! Solomon gave her everything she asked for. Then she went home. She was a queen and her country needed her.

The ships kept bringing gold and almond trees from Ophir. Solomon transplanted the trees by the temple and by his palace.

There was nobody as rich or as wise as Solomon in the world at that time. Solomon had fourteen hundred chariots and twelve thousand horsemen.

He did everything in excess! But Solomon also had seven hundred wives and three hundred concubines from all the countries and tribes around him. God had told the people they were not to intermarry with those who served other gods; but Solomon used marriage as a way to keep peace among his neighbors. Each one of the wives brought along her gods. For many of the wives, Solomon built palaces.

In his old age, his wives turned his heart away from God, and he began to worship other gods with them. He even built a high place for Chemosh, the detestable god of the Moabites, and for Molech, the equally detestable god of the Ammonites. The worship of these false gods involved child sacrifice.

God told Solomon that because he had not continued to serve Him as his father David had, He was going to take the kingdom away from Solomon's son when he should have had it. God would take ten tribes and give them to another; but He was going to leave one tribe, for His servant David's sake.

Enemies began to rise up out of the countries over which Solomon reigned. Jeroboam was a mighty man whom Solomon had put in charge of the tribe of Joseph. When Solomon heard that Ahijah the prophet had told Jeroboam he was to get ten tribes, Solomon tried to kill him, but Jeroboam escaped to Egypt.

Solomon reigned for forty years. Then he died and was buried in the city of David.

Solomon's son, Rehoboam, followed him on the throne.

Rehoboam, Solomon's son, was a wimp. He didn't have wisdom like Solomon had. He didn't have God on his side. His mother was a Sidonian, so he had bad training, and he worshipped the Baals. He was not a hero; in fact, he was a failure in every way.

Rehoboam

As soon as Jeroboam heard that Solomon was dead, he came back to Israel. He and all the people came and talked to Rehoboam, the new king. They told him, "Your father put heavy taxes on us. We are tired of all the taxes. If you will take away some of these awful taxes, we will serve you and you can be our king."

The old advisors told him to listen to them; but Rehoboam listened to the advice of the young men around him.

He told the people, "No. My father's taxes were small compared to what mine will be. I will make your taxes even greater than they are, now."

The people rebelled and made Jeroboam king over the ten tribes of Israel. Only Judah and Benjamin stayed with Rehoboam.

The kingdom was divided and never got back together, again.

The Divided Kingdom

Now Jeroboam was afraid that the people would return to Judah because the altar and the temple were in Jerusalem. He made two calves of gold and put one in Bethel and the other in Dan. So, there was one at each end of the country. He told the people it was too much trouble for them to go all the way to Jerusalem to worship. Then he made an altar and sacrificed there. He made priests of those who were not priests. This thing became a sin to the nation.

God sent a man from Judah to tell Jeroboam how wrong he was about the altar. Jeroboam put his hand out to strike the man of God. His hand dried up, so that he could not move it. When Jeroboam asked the man of God to pray for his healing, he did, and the Lord restored his hand.

Jeroboam asked him to come home with him, saying that he would give him a reward. The man of God told him, "No, I will not go home with you, or eat or drink in this place, because God told me not to; and I am to go home another way." So he set out to obey the Lord.

Now there was an old prophet in Bethel. When he heard what the man of God had done and what he had told the king, he went after him and invited him to come to his house.

The young man told him what God had said about not eating or drinking anything in that place; but the old prophet lied to him and said that the Lord had told him that it was all right for him to come home with him and eat bread.

While they were eating, the old prophet told him that God was going to judge him for disobedience. When the young prophet started for home again, a lion met him and killed him.

The old prophet went and got his body and buried it in his own tomb and mourned over him. He told his sons that when he died, they were to bury him next to the young prophet because God was surely going to do all the young prophet had said He would.

Lesson: Mind God, not people! People can lie; God never does!

Ruler after ruler reigned in both countries. Most of them did evil in the sight of the Lord.

Asa reigned over Judah for forty-one years. He did what was right in the eyes of the Lord. He tore down all the altars to strange gods and burned them. He was a builder, like Solomon was, but he stayed true to the Lord all the days of his life. ASA WAS A HERO.

There was war between the two countries, Israel and Judah, all the days of Asa. He died, and Jehoshaphat, his son, reigned in his place.

The kings of the Northern Kingdom, Israel, were bad and worse, each of them repeating the sins of their fathers, and worse. There was just one king after another who did evil.

Omri came along, and did evil. He had a son, Ahab, who reigned after him. Ahab was the most wicked of all. He had a wife named Jezebel, the daughter of the king of the Sidonians. She was a Baal worshipper, so Ahab became one, too. He made an altar and a grove for Baal in Samaria, and worshipped him, there.

Elijah was a prophet of God. He obeyed God in every way. God used him in such a mighty way that we still remember how he was able to call down fire from heaven, to show who God was to his people. Elijah was a hero worth following!

Elijah

God sent a man named Elijah to Ahab with a message. He told Ahab there would not be dew or rain in Israel for years, until he said so.

Then God told Elijah, "Go and hide by the brook Kerith. I have told the ravens to feed you and you can drink from the brook." Ravens came every morning and every night.

After awhile, with no rain, the brook dried up. God told Elijah to go to Zarephath, where He had commanded a widow lady to take care of him, so Elijah went.

When he got there, he found the lady out gathering sticks. He asked her for a drink of water and a morsel of bread. She told him she was gathering sticks to make a little loaf for herself and her son with the very last of the meal she had. Then they would die of starvation.

Elijah told her, "Make a little cake for me, first; then you will have enough to make one for yourself and your son, because the meal and the oil will not run out. The Lord has promised."

The lady did exactly as he told her to do. Just as God had promised, the meal was always there and so was the oil. God just kept supplying it as long as Elijah was there. God was taking care of all three of them.

This went on for some time. One day, the son got very sick and died. The woman thought it was because of her sin---that God was punishing her.

Elijah took the little boy up into his loft room, laid him on his bed and began to pray over him. He lay over the child and God restored him to life. Elijah took him back to his mother.

The woman declared, "Now I know that you are a man of God and what you say is from the Lord."

It had been over three years since it had rained when God told Elijah, "It is time to go back and talk to Ahab; I am ready to send rain on the land."

There was such a terrible drought that even the king and his servant, Obadiah, were out looking for just a bit of grass to feed his horses and mules, to keep them alive.

Now the king didn't know it, but Obadiah had hidden a hundred prophets of the Lord in caves, to save their lives from murder by Jezebel. As Elijah came back from Zarephath, the first one he saw was Obadiah. He told Obadiah, "Go to the king and tell him that I am here and I want to see him."

Obadiah was terrified. He said, "King Ahab has looked for you in every country around. All of them swore that Elijah was not there. Now, if I tell him Elijah is here, and the Spirit of the Lord catches you up and puts you somewhere else, Ahab will certainly kill me."

Elijah promised that he would be there to meet King Ahab, and he was.

Ahab's first words to Elijah, were, "Are you the one who troubles Israel?"

Elijah told him, "I'm not the one; you are, because you have turned your back on God and are worshipping the Baals."

Then Elijah told Ahab, "Call all the prophets of Baal, bring them and meet me at Mount Carmel." Elijah and all the people went to Mount Carmel.

Elijah told them, "It is time to decide who you will worship. The prophets of Baal will make an altar; and I will make an altar to the Lord. Neither of us will set fire to our sacrifice. We will call upon our God to light the fire under his sacrifice. The God who answers by fire will be your God." (Baal was supposed to be the fire god).

The people all said, "Wonderful!" (If nothing else, it should be a great show).

So, the 850 prophets of Baal put their altar together, dressed their bullock, put it on the altar, and began to call upon their god to send down fire. Since they were not to put any fire on the altar they had to wait for their god to light it with his fire.

All day long, they called on Baal. They danced, shouted, even cut themselves to get his attention.

Elijah taunted them by telling them, "Maybe he is asleep or on a journey and can't hear you. Call louder." So they danced and shouted even louder. But there was no answer. No one heard. There was no one there and no one to care.

At the time of the evening sacrifice, Elijah called all the people over to him. He had taken a long time to build the altar of the Lord, using twelve stones to represent the twelve tribes of Israel the Lord had brought out of Egyptian slavery.

He had dug a deep trench around the altar, put the wood in order, and the bullock on it. Then he had them pour twelve barrels of precious water all over it, until it soaked the wood, ran over and filled the trench.

Then Elijah prayed a simple prayer to God, asking, "Let these people know that I am doing all this at your command, that you want them to know that only you are God, and you are turning your people back to yourself."

THEN, THE FIRE FROM GOD FELL AND BURNT UP THE SACRIFICE, THE WOOD, THE STONES, THE DUST, AND LICKED UP ALL THE WATER THAT WAS IN THE TRENCH!

The people fell on their faces and cried out, "The Lord, He is God! The Lord, He is God!"

Elijah told them to kill all the prophets of Baal, not to let a one of them escape. They did.

Then Elijah told Ahab to hurry and eat his supper because there was a sound of a great rain coming. So Ahab went and had his supper on the mountain.

Elijah went up to the top of the mountain, fell on his face, and began to pray. He told his servant to go look toward the sea. Six times, the servant saw nothing. The seventh time, he came back and said, "There is a little cloud the size of a man's hand coming out of the sea."

Elijah sent him to Ahab to tell the king, "Hurry down off the mountain because there is a huge rain coming."

Suddenly, the sky was black with clouds and wind, and it began to pour. Ahab rode his chariot as fast as he could drive it. But the Spirit of the Lord came on Elijah and he ran in front of the chariot all the way down the mountain to Jezreel.

When he got home, Ahab told Jezebel what had happened and what Elijah had done. She did not see the miracle God had done or want to hear about it. She was furious that Elijah had killed her prophets. She sent word to Elijah that by this time tomorrow he would be as dead as her prophets were!

Elijah knew Jezebel. He was afraid of this wicked woman! He ran for his life.

He took his servant with him and they ran the entire length of the country into Judah until they came to Beersheba. His servant was exhausted, so he left him there.

Elijah went another day out into the wilderness. He finally ran out of steam and found a juniper tree and sat down and fell asleep under it. He was so tired and discouraged that he told God to take his life. (Of course, if he had really wanted to die, all he had to do was wait for Jezebel to do the job).

An angel came to him as he slept under the juniper tree, woke him and told him to get up and eat. There was a cake baked on a little fire and a jar of water. He ate and drank and fell asleep again.

The angel came a second time and told him, "Eat and drink. The journey is too hard for you."

He got up, ate and drank. Then he went for forty days and nights until he got to Mt. Horeb, the Mountain of God. He spent the night in a cave, there. The Lord spoke to him and asked him, "What are you doing here, Elijah?"

Elijah answered, "I have done everything you told me to do; but the Children of Israel have not kept your covenant. They have killed your prophets and thrown down your altars. I am the only one left serving you. And they are trying to kill me!"

God told him, "Go out and stand on the top of the mountain because the Lord is passing by."

A great, strong wind came, breaking rocks, but the Lord was not in the wind. After the wind, there was an earthquake, then a fire, but the Lord was not in the earthquake or the fire. And after the fire there was a still, small voice. When Elijah heard it, he wrapped his mantle around him, went out and stood at the mouth of the cave, and God came and talked with him.

He asked him, again, what he was doing there. Elijah told him again about them trying to kill him and that only he was left serving God.

God told him, "I have seven thousand in Israel who have not bowed the knee to Baal or kissed him."

Then God gave Elijah some assignments. He was to anoint Hazael king over Syria, Jehu king over Israel, and Elisha to be prophet after himself. Each one would do his job and God would be glorified. So, Elijah left the cave and went to do God's bidding.

First, he found Elisha, who was out in the field plowing with twelve yoke of oxen, himself driving the twelfth pair (someone with the physical strength of Elijah). Elijah threw his mantle over Elisha to show that he was chosen.

Elisha left his oxen and ran after Elijah. He said, "Let me go home and tell them where I am going; then I will follow you."

Elisha went home, took a yoke of the oxen, killed them and cooked them over a fire he made out of the farming equipment, a sign that he was done farming. Then he fed the people with the cooked oxen. He went after Elijah and was his servant all the days of Elijah.

Naboth's Vineyard

A man named Naboth had a vineyard in Jezreel, which was next to King Ahab's house. Ahab wanted it. He tried to buy it from Naboth, but Naboth would not sell because it was part of his inheritance from the Lord and had long been in his family.

Ahab went home and pouted. His wife, Jezebel, told him, "Cheer up, I will get the vineyard for you."

She wrote letters in Ahab's name to the elders and nobles in the city.

She told them, "Declare a fast, ask Naboth to come, have two men hired to lie about him saying that he blasphemed God and the king. Then, carry him out and stone him to death." The men of the city did as the queen told them to do.

When she heard that Naboth was dead, she told Ahab that he could have his vineyard because Naboth was dead. Ahab went down to take possession of the vineyard.

God told Elijah to go meet Ahab in the vineyard. Elijah was to tell him, "Have you killed and now take possession? In the place where dogs licked up the blood of Naboth, shall dogs lick up your blood." Elijah told him, "Because you have determined to do evil, God will bring evil upon you. Every last male in your household will be cut off and consumed."

Ahab went to Jehoshaphat, king of Judah, and talked him into joining him in going to war. Micaiah, a prophet, warned them that God said they would be defeated; but they didn't listen to him.

Ahab disguised himself, thinking they wouldn't recognize him and try to kill him. But a soldier wounded him, anyway. Ahab turned his chariot around and went back to Jezreel. He died in the chariot and his blood filled it. They washed it in the pool and the dogs licked up the blood, just as Elijah had predicted.

Elijah's Chariot of Fire

Now, Elijah had set up prophet schools. He had a circuit he traveled every year visiting the prophets.

Elisha knew God was going to take Elijah to heaven that day, but neither of them said anything about it. At each place, Elijah told Elisha to stay. Elisha told him he would not leave him, so they both went along, together.

The sons of the prophets all knew the Lord would be taking Elijah away that day, too, and told Elisha. He replied, "Yes, I know it. Keep quiet about it."

Finally, Elijah and Elisha got to the Jordan River. Elijah took his mantle, struck the water and the Jordan opened up a path. They went over on dry ground.

Elijah asked Elisha what he wanted him to do for him before he left. Elisha said, "I want a double portion of your spirit."

Elijah told him, "That is a hard thing that you ask, but if you see me leave, you will get what you want."

Suddenly, a chariot of fire swooped down, pulled by horses of fire and flew between them. Elijah went up to heaven in a whirlwind as Elisha watched. Elijah's mantle fell to the ground. Elisha picked it up. He had lost his master and beloved friend, but WHAT A WAY TO GO!!

Elisha stood by the bank of the river, struck the river with Elijah's mantle, and said, "Where is the God of Elijah?" The water opened just as it had for Elijah. Elisha went back across on dry land.

Elisha was a prophet of God who stayed true all his life. Where Elijah had the faith to call down fire from heaven, Elisha had the faith to help people--in strange ways--but help them, he did. Elisha was a hero.

Elisha

Fifty men of the prophets were standing there watching as Elisha came back over the river. They told him they could see that the Spirit of Elijah was on Elisha.

They wanted to go and search for Elijah's body. Elisha told them,"No," but they finally got his permission and went, anyway.

They looked for three days and found nothing. Elisha said, "I told you so."

The first miracle of Elisha was to heal the waters of a city so that they no longer brought death or barren land.

He was not a pushover, though. As he was going up to Bethel, a bunch of juvenile delinquents came after him, yelling, "Go up, you bald head. Go up, you bald head!" (They were saying that the story of Elijah going up in a whirlwind was a lie; that God didn't do what He did, and they wouldn't believe Elisha). Elisha cursed them in the name of the Lord. Soon after, two she bears came out of the woods and mauled forty-two of them.

A widow of one of the prophets came to Elisha. She told him that her husband had been a good, godly man; but he had debts before he died. Now the men to whom he owed money were going to take her two sons as slaves, to pay the debt.

Elisha asked her, "What do you have in the house?"

She said, "Nothing but a small jug of oil."

Elisha told her, "Send your sons out and have them borrow every empty jar and jug they can find. Get a lot of them! Bring them all into the house, shut the door, then pour from your little jug until all the jars are full. After that, take the jars and sell them, pay the debts, and live on the rest of the money." She did what he said and saved her sons. The oil had kept flowing until every jar was full.

There was another woman, a wealthy woman, who noticed every time Elisha walked past her house, which was often. She decided he needed a place to stop and rest, so she made a little room on the top of her house for him.

He had his servant, Gehazi, call the woman and ask her what he could do for her. She said she needed nothing. Elisha asked Gehazi what could be done for her. His response was that the woman had no child and her husband was old.

Elisha told her, "By next year you will have a son." She and her husband were elated! They had given up on being able to have children.

After awhile, as the little boy got bigger, he went out with his father into the fields with the reapers one day. He stayed too long and got sunstroke. His head hurt so his father had him taken home to his mother. She held him all morning, but about noon, he died.

She took his body up to the room she had made for Elisha and laid him on the bed. She told her husband that she was going to see the man of God. She had a donkey saddled for herself, took the servant and raced to Carmel to find Elisha.

He saw her coming a ways off and sent Gehazi to see what she wanted; but she would not tell Gehazi. When she got to Elisha, she told him about her little boy dying. He sent Gehazi to lay his staff on the boy's face; but the mother would not leave without Elisha.

So, Elisha hurried to her house with her. He saw that the child was dead. He went into his bedroom and shut the door. He lay upon the child, gave him mouth to mouth and eye to eye. He rubbed the child and prayed over him. Finally the child sneezed seven times and opened his eyes. Elisha called the Shunammite woman and gave her son back to her. She fell at his feet in thanksgiving.

Another time, Elisha was eating with the sons of the prophets, when one of them accidentally put some poisonous gourds into the pot of food. Elisha put in some meal and there was no harm in the food.

Another time, he multiplied food that had been given by a generous man, but was not enough to feed the multitude. There was food left over.

Naaman

Now Naaman was captain of the army of the king of Syria. He was a great man, honorable in all he did, a mighty man of valor, but he was a leper.

He had a little maid who had been taken captive from Israel. She served Naaman's wife. Naaman's wife loved this little girl and the girl loved her masters. She told them, "If only my master, Naaman, were with the prophet that is in Samaria, he would heal him of his leprosy." This little girl knew God and His prophet and believed.

When the king of Syria heard about it, he was delighted that there was someone who could heal his captain of leprosy! He didn't know it was impossible at that time!

The king of Syria sent Naaman to Samaria to the king of Israel. He took many wonderful gifts.

But when he got to the king of Israel, the king tore his clothes, he was so upset. He thought they were trying to force him into battle, because he knew that he could not heal leprosy! Nobody could!

When Elisha heard about it, he sent word to the king. "Send the man to me and they will know that there is a prophet of God in Israel."

Naaman went to Elisha. When he got to Elisha's house with all his chariots and horsemen and pride, Elisha didn't even come to the door to greet him. He sent word by his servant, telling Naaman, "Go and wash in the Jordan River seven times and you will be healed."

Naaman got angry. He had expected Elisha to come out, wave his hand over him, call on his God and heal him.

He went away mad! He said, "The rivers of Damascus are far better than this old, dirty Jordan River. I will not lower myself to wash in this muddy Jordan!"

His wise servant came to Naaman and said, "If he had told you to do some hard thing, wouldn't you have done it? How much better to just go and wash in this river and be clean."

That made sense. So Naaman changed his mind, and went and washed in the Jordan River. He dipped himself in it seven times. The seventh time, he came up healed.

He hurried back to Elisha to thank him. He told him that now he knew there was no God like the God of Israel, who could heal something like leprosy. He had many gifts he wanted to give to Elisha, but Elisha would accept none of them.

So, Naaman asked for the dirt that two mules could carry, because he said, "I will make a worship center for myself with the soil and worship only the Lord God, from now on."

He asked the Lord to pardon him when he had to go into the temple of Rimmon with his king when the king was worshipping, because it was his job. Elisha said it was all right. God understood.

Naaman started home. He hadn't gotten far, when Gehazi, Elisha's servant, came running after him.

Gehazi lied and told him that two young prophets had come, and Elisha wanted a talent of gold and two changes of clothes for them. Naaman gave him two talents of gold and the clothing and sent two men to carry them for him.

When they got near his place, Gehazi sent the men back, hid the money and clothes in his house, then went back to Elisha, pretending he hadn't been anywhere.

Elisha knew what he had done, and told him, "Didn't my heart break when I saw you going to the man and taking credit for what God did for him? It made God look bad. Because of what you did, Naaman's leprosy will come upon you for the rest of your life." Gehazi left Elisha, a leper, white as snow.

The prophets needed a larger place, so they set out to build one. One of them borrowed an axe. As he was working with it, the iron axe head fell off, landed in the water and disappeared. He felt badly because it wasn't even his own; he had borrowed it. When he told Elisha, Elisha tossed a wooden stick into the water where the axe head had fallen. The iron floated. They picked it up and put it back on its handle.

Syria

The king of Syria went to war against Israel. Everything he planned, Elisha told the king of Israel. Elisha warned the Israelite king of places not to go, where the Syrians would be. Every ambush Syria planned was thwarted by Elisha.

The Syrian king began to suspect his own men of being spies for Israel. One of his men told him that it was Elisha.

The king sent a whole army of soldiers to the town of Dothan, where Elisha was, to arrest him and bring him back to Syria.

When they got up the next morning, Elisha's servant was horrified to see that they were completely surrounded by the Syrian army. He knew that they had come for Elisha.

Elisha told him, "Don't be afraid. There are more on our side than on theirs." Then he prayed, "Lord, open the eyes of this young man so he can see." God opened his eyes, and the young man saw that the mountains were full of horses and chariots of fire all around Elisha.

Elisha prayed for God to strike the army with blindness. God did. Then Elisha went out to them and told them that they were in the wrong place. He led them to Samaria, where Israel's king was. Then he had their eyes opened; they suddenly realized they were in enemy territory.

Israel's king wanted to kill them, but Elisha had him feed them, instead, and send them home. They went home and when their king saw the kindness of Israel he quit making war against them.

Elisha sent one of the prophets to Ramoth Gilead, where Jehu was. He told him to call Jehu off by himself, anoint him to be king over Israel in place of Ahab's sons, then run away as fast as he could.

The young prophet did as he was told.

Jehu called his men together and went to Jezreel and declared himself king.

Wicked Queen Mother, Jezebel, was watching out a window as he rode by. He told the men up there with her to throw her out. They did. By the time Jehu sent to pick up her body, the dogs had eaten it, just like Elijah had said they would, because of her wickedness.

Jehu had all the sons of Ahab killed and all the followers of Baal. He tore down Baal's altars and burned them. But he did not get rid of the golden calves in Bethel and Dan.

Elisha got sick and died. They buried him in a tomb. Once while some Israelites were burying a dead man, a band of Moabite raiders came by. In haste, the Israelites threw the body into Elisha's tomb. When it touched the bones of Elisha, the man revived and walked away. So, even in death, Elisha gave life.

King after king reigned in Judah and Israel, most of them fighting against each other and the nations around them. Most of them did evil in the sight of the Lord, but a few served Him faithfully and helped their people to do so. Whatever the king did, that was what the people did.

A long time later, Hezekiah became ruler in Judah. He reigned for twenty-nine years. He did exactly what was right in the sight of the Lord, all his life. There was none like him, before or after. He was a hero worth following.

He tore down the high places in Judah where people had been worshipping false gods for generations. He removed every trace of idolatry he could find, and led the nation in worshipping the true God. The Lord was with him.

But Hezekiah and the Southern Kingdom of Judah had a bad enemy, Assyria. The king of Assyria had already conquered the people of the Northern Kingdom,Israel, taken them out of their land and dragged them off to Assyria as captives. Now, he had captured the walled cities of Judah. His army surrounded Jerusalem, the capital, to take it. He sent messengers to Hezekiah to get him to come out and surrender.

They yelled at the people who watched from the wall, "We are going to take this city. No other god has been able to defend a city against us, so what makes you think your God can! Your God is useless to defend you."

Hezekiah had told the people that God would defend them. They believed him and didn't say anything to the messengers.

When Hezekiah got a letter from Sennacherib, king of Assyria, he took it to the temple and laid it before the Lord. He prayed, "Protect us, Oh God. Only you can protect us from this mighty army. Please do it to show the whole world that you are the only God and that we are your people."

Isaiah, the prophet, sent to tell Hezekiah, "God has heard your prayer. God is going to deliver the city of David and things will get better. The king of Assyria will go home knowing that the Lord has the power, not he."

That night the angel of the Lord went out and struck the camp of the Assyrians. The next morning, almost the whole camp of Sennacherib lay dead. So Sennacherib went home to Nineveh, defeated by God. He never returned.

For years God sent prophet after prophet to Judah to try to get them to repent and turn back to Him, but they had deaf ears and refused to listen. Finally, God let them be captured by Nebuchadnezzar, king of Babylon, to punish them and bring them back to Himself.

Esther was a young lady, actually just a girl, who had the wisdom and courage to do whatever was needed to save her people, and she did. She is a hero who is still honored by her people, yet today.

When God had had enough of their following other gods, He allowed Judah to be conquered by Nebuchadnezar . They were kept captive for about 70 years. After that time, the people were allowed to go back to Jerusalem, many did, but a lot of the people of Judah, who were taken captive to Babylon, settled down there and made good homes for themselves and their families. Some, like Daniel and his three friends, even rose to great positions in the government of Babylon. Esther was one of these--a girl who became queen in a foreign country.

Esther

This is a story of one such person who became very great, and even saved her people, far beyond the borders of the city where she lived.

Her name was Hadassah. She was a little Jewish girl. Her parents had died when she was very young, so a relative, her cousin Mordecai, had taken her in and raised her. She was like a daughter to him. She trusted and obeyed him like she would have obeyed and loved her father.

Her Babylonian name was Esther. Because Mordecai wanted to protect her, he called her Esther, and told her not to tell anyone she was Jewish. Esther obeyed him.

The great king, Xerxes, gave a banquet at his palace in Susa for all his princes, noblemen and political and military officials from all the provinces .He wanted to show off his wealth and his mighty power. He wanted to do a lot of bragging, and he did! For 180 days, all his wealth and power were on display. King Xerxes finished up with a week-long feast in the royal garden.

The women were feasting, too. Queen Vashti had invited them all to the palace.

Everybody who wanted to was drinking as much as they wanted. The king had drunk more than he should have, and was not thinking well. He decided to call the queen to come in so he could show her off as the greatest of his possessions. Vashti was very beautiful.

She was to wear her crown, all her jewels, and parade in front of the men. Xerxes sent seven of his chamberlains to order Vashti to come to his banquet. Vashti refused to come.

This made the king very angry. After all, this was a time when men ruled the entire world. Women did what men told them to do. They did not think for themselves, ever! (Or if they did, they kept it quiet).

The king was so angry he asked his advisors what they should do to Queen Vashti for her rebellion.

His wise men answered, "Vashti has disgraced not only the king but every man in the nation. If she goes unpunished, every woman in the world will think she can disobey her husband. There will be anarchy! Vashti should be divorced as queen, put away, and another one should be given her place. The king should write the pronouncement according to the laws of the Medes and Persians, so it can't be changed. Then all the wives will honor their husbands, both great and small."

The king followed their advice and wrote the law. He sent copies of the law to every part of the nation.

When the king finally calmed down and got sober, he thought about Vashti and felt sorry for what he had decreed. His advisors noticed it and made a suggestion. They said that he should appoint officers in all the kingdom to find beautiful young virgin girls in their area, bring them to Susa, let them spend time getting ready, then be brought to the king for a night. He could choose the one he liked best for a new queen. That sounded enticing to the king, so that is what he did.

When the king's commandment and decree were announced, Esther was one of the very beautiful young ladies chosen to go to Susa as a prospective bride for the king. When Esther was taken, Mordecai followed after.

Every day he walked by the court of the women so Esther could see he was there and would not be afraid; and he could be sure she was all right. He did this, day after day, for many months.

Every girl had to be there for twelve months for her purification: six months with oil of myrrh and six months with perfumes and cosmetics. Then, each one went to the king for a night. She could take anything she wanted to take along with her. She went at night; the next morning, she went to the second house of the women where she stayed forever as a concubine of the king. She never went back to the king, again, unless he called for her by name.

When it came Esther's time to go to the king, all she took with her was what was suggested by Hegai, the king's chamberlain, who liked Esther. In fact, everyone who saw Esther liked her. They all admired her sweet spirit.

The king, Xerxes, immediately liked her, too. In fact, she pleased him more than any of the others who had been there before her. He chose Esther to be his new queen. The king made a great feast for her. He called it Esther's Feast.

Mordecai sat in the gate of the king, still keeping track of Esther. One day, he heard two of the king's chamberlains plotting to kill the king. He sent word and told it to Esther, who informed the king of the danger. She told the king that Mordecai was the one to be thanked for saving him. The two chamberlains were found guilty and hanged.

About this time, the king promoted a man named Haman, an Agagite, to be his head official. Everybody bowed and scraped to Haman except Mordecai. Mordecai wouldn't bow to him. All the others made special effort to mention it to Haman that Mordecai did not bow to him because he was a Jew.

Haman was furious. He felt that he was worthy of every knee bowing to him. If Jews wouldn't bow to him, he wanted to destroy all of them.

Haman went to King Xerxes and told him there were certain people in his kingdom whose laws were different from his. "They don't keep the king's laws," he said, "and it would be better for the king to get rid of all of them."

The king didn't question him about it, especially after Haman offered to pay ten thousand talents of silver to the king's treasury if Xerxes would write a law for them to be destroyed. The king took off his ring and gave it to Haman. He said Haman could do whatever he wanted with the people.

Haman and his friends cast lots to decide in which month to kill all the Jews. Then he had letters sent to every province in the realm of Babylon--almost the whole world at that time.

The letters said they were to destroy, kill, wipe out all men, women, babies, little children and old people in one day, who were of the Jewish nation. It was all to happen on the thirteenth day of the twelfth month, Adar.

Those who killed them could take their lands for their own; and the Jews were not even to try to defend themselves.

The letters went out. The King and Haman sat down to drink, and all the Jews, especially those in Susa, wondered what was going on and what had happened to bring all this on.

When Mordecai heard the bad news, he tore his clothes, put on sack cloth and ashes, and cried. He went and sat outside the king's gate, weeping. All over the country, other Jews were behaving the same way.

Esther's maids came and told her about Mordecai. She sent clothes out to him but he refused to take them. So, Esther sent her trusted servant, Hathach, out to ask him what was the matter.

Mordecai told him all about Haman's treachery, and how the Jews were to be destroyed. He gave him a copy of the decree to give to Esther. He said to tell Esther she should go to the king and make a plea for her people.

When Esther heard it, she said to tell Mordecai that she had not been called to the king for thirty days; and anybody who went to the king without being called was killed, unless the king reached out his golden scepter to them.

Mordecai sent word back to Esther: "Don't think you will escape, just because you are in the palace. If you don't speak up now, God will raise up someone else to save his people, but you and your house will perish. And who knows, maybe this is why you are queen at this time."

Esther sent back word, "Gather all the Jews together that are in Susa, and fast and pray for me. Don't eat or drink anything for three days. I and my maidens will do the same. Then I will go to the king, even though it is against the law. And if I die, I die."

So, Mordecai and all the Jews in Susa did what she had told them to do.

On the third day, Esther dressed in all her royal clothing and went to the king's court. She stood in the inner court, looking as beautiful as she could. The king sat on his royal throne. When he looked out, there was his queen, standing there. He was pleased and held out the royal scepter to her. So, Esther came up to him and touched the tip of the scepter.

The king asked, "What does my lovely queen want? I will give her anything she asks for."

Esther invited him and Haman to a banquet that night, if he would so honor her. Then she would tell him. "Of course," he said. "Yes, they would come."

That night, Esther still did not tell the king what her request was, but she asked him and Haman to come again, the next night. They agreed.

When he heard it, Haman was thrilled to death. He left, walking on air, but when he got out by the gate he saw Mordecai, who didn't bow to him or even act like he saw him. It punctured his balloon.

Haman ignored it, but when he got home, he called his friends and bragged about all his riches, and the fact that only he had been invited to attend a banquet with the king, at the queen's palace-- two nights in a row! Then, he added that all this didn't please him, because there was Mordecai sitting at the king's gate, refusing to bow to him!

His wife and friends suggested that he should build a gallows 75 feet high, and tomorrow he should speak to the king and ask for Mordecai to be hanged on it. So, Haman had the gallows built.

That night the king could not sleep. He had the records brought in and read to him. There he found the record of Mordecai saving his life. When he asked what had been done for Mordecai, they said, "Nothing."

It was early in the morning. The king asked, "Who is in the courtyard?" He was told that Haman had just come in, so he had them send Haman in to him.

When Haman came in the king asked him, "What should be done to honor a man whom the king delights to honor? "

Haman thought, "Who would the king want to honor more than me?"

So he told the king, "Let him wear a robe the king has worn, ride on one of the king's royal horses, and have one of the highest nobles lead him through the city calling, 'This is what shall be done for the man the king delights to honor.'"

The king told Haman, "Go quickly, and do all you have said for Mordecai, the Jew, who sits at the king's gate."

Haman did as the king had commanded. Then he took Mordecai back to the gate, but he went home with his head covered. He told his wife and all his friends everything. They all told him that he was in deep trouble since Mordecai was a Jew and had been so honored!

While he was still bemoaning his fate, the king's chamberlain came to take him to Esther's banquet. He hurried up and went.

When they had eaten, the king asked again, "What is it you want, Queen Esther? Whatever it is, I will give it to you."

Esther answered, "If I have found favor in your sight, let my life be given to me, and that of my people. For we are about to be killed. If it had only been that we would be sold as slaves, I would not have said anything."

The king demanded, "Who dares to do such a thing?!"

Esther said, "The enemy is this wicked Haman!"

Haman was terrified in front of the king and the queen. The king went out into the garden because he was so angry. He had to think what to do.

Haman thought he must beg for his life. The queen was reclining on a couch, and Haman fell upon the couch, begging.

Just then the king came back in. He was furious. He shouted, "Will you now try to molest the queen?!"

As soon as the king spoke, his attendants covered Haman's face. One of the servants told the king about the gallows Haman had made at his house, where he had planned to hang good Mordecai.

The king ordered, "Hang him on it!" So they hanged Haman on the gallows he had prepared for Mordecai.

The king gave Haman's property to Esther. Esther told him who Mordecai was to her; and the king took off his ring that had been

Haman's and gave it to Mordecai. Esther set Mordecai over Haman's property.

Then Esther fell down at the king's feet and begged for her people. She begged him to reverse the law that had been written.

The king said that the writing could not be reversed, but he gave permission to Mordecai to add to it anything he could and send it out as a decree.

Mordecai added. "Every Jew is to arm himself and protect all he owns and all his people. He can kill anyone who tries to harm him or his family on the day announced in the former edict; and the Jews may plunder the property of their enemies.

So Mordecai went out from the presence of the king in royal apparel of blue and white, with a great crown of gold, a garment of fine linen and purple, and the city of Susa rejoiced and was glad.

The Jews had feast days in every city where the proclamation came, throughout the whole empire.

On the appointed day, many helped the Jews. Their enemies were now afraid of them, and the Jews prevailed, now that they were able to defend themselves and their property. The Jews ended up killing many of their enemies, but although the Jews had been given permission to take the property of their enemies, they didn't.

Mordecai's fame spread throughout the land. Mordecai and Esther sent out a decree to all Jews everywhere, that "from this day on, all Jews are to rejoice and keep the Feast of Purim."

The "lot" used as a kind of dice was known as the "pur." That's why they chose this name for the Feast of Purim---because of the pur (lot) cast against the Jews, when Haman chose in which month they would be destroyed---but when God used two of His heroes, Queen Esther and her cousin Mordecai to save His people.

Our next heroes are four young men who were taken as prisoners from their home in Judah to Babylon, a foreign country, because they were promising young men. Nebuchadnezzar didn't realize what jewels he had stolen for a long time, but eventually he did. These four young men are real heroes. They stayed true to their God, no matter what! They eventually showed the king who was really God, and converted him. Daniel wrote about it in a book for us to read in the Bible

Daniel

Some of the first ones to be taken to Babylon when Judah fell were the young princes, good looking children of wisdom and talent, good in mathematics, and those who had ability to learn the Chaldean language.

They were put in a special place, with guards to oversee them. Among these were four friends: Daniel, Hananiah, Mishael and Azariah. The chief official changed their names to: Belteshazzar, Shadrach, Meshach and Abednego.

Daniel and his friends had determined in their hearts that they would not defile themselves by eating food from the king's table, so Daniel asked the chief official, who really liked him, to let them have just vegetables and water to drink.

Even though the official liked Daniel and his friends, he was afraid of what would happen to him if he didn't follow orders, so he declined.

Then Daniel asked the guard whom the chief official had appointed over them if he would give them a ten day trial of just vegetables and water, then see how they looked, compared to the other kids. If he and his friends weren't looking better than the others, they would eat the king's food and drink his wine. The guard agreed.

After the trial period, Daniel and his friends looked far better than the ones who were eating the king's rich food and drinking his wine; so the guard let them continue eating vegetables and drinking water.

God gave these four young men knowledge and skill in all learning and wisdom; and Daniel could interpret dreams and visions.

A few years later, when they finally stood before the king, they showed that they were ten times wiser than all the astrologers and magicians in the king's realm.

After a year or so, Nebuchadnezzar had a disturbing dream, but he couldn't remember it. He called all his astrologers and magicians in to have them tell him the dream and the interpretation of it.

They were horrified! "Nobody can do that!" they told him. "You must tell us the dream, first."

The king was so angry that he commanded that all of the wise men in his kingdom should be killed!

When they came for Daniel and his friends, Daniel wanted to know what was going on and what was the big hurry?

Then Daniel went to Nebuchadnezzar and asked him to give him more time. He said that he would show him the dream and the meaning.

Then he and his three friends went to prayer about it. That night, God gave Daniel the dream and the meaning. Daniel praised the God of Heaven for being so kind to his servants to help them and to spare everybody's lives.

The next day, Daniel went to the king. First, he told him, "Nobody can do this except the God who makes all things and reveals secrets. It is only God who could tell me the dream and the meaning for the king." He put himself down and glorified God. He said that nobody else could do what God does.

Then he told Nebuchadnezzar the dream: "You saw a great image. It was very bright. Its head was fine gold, its breast and arms were silver, its belly and thighs of brass, its legs of iron, and its feet were part iron and part clay. A stone cut without hands hit the clay and iron feet and broke them to pieces, and the whole image fell and broke and blew away, while the stone became a great mountain that filled the whole earth. "

"That was the dream. And here is the interpretation of it:

"You, oh king, are the head, for the God of heaven has given you a kingdom, and power, and strength, and glory. After you will rise another kingdom inferior to you; then a third kingdom of brass, which will be over all the earth. The fourth kingdom will be strong as iron, breaking and bruising; but the kingdom will be divided, partly strong like iron and partly broken like clay. In those days, the God of Heaven will set up a kingdom which shall never be destroyed. It will break in pieces and eat up all these kingdoms, and it will stand forever.

You saw the stone that was cut out of the mountain without hands. It will break the iron, the brass, the silver, and the gold."

"The great God of Heaven has made known to King Nebuchadnezzar what will be; and it is a sure thing. It will be a long time coming, but it is going to happen."

Then the king fell on his face before Daniel and said, "It is true. Your God is a God of gods, and a Lord of kings and a revealer of secrets, seeing how you could reveal this secret to me."

Then the king promoted Daniel, gave him many gifts and made him ruler over the whole province of Babylon and all the wise men of Babylon.

At Daniel's request, his three friends were made administrators over the province of Babylon, but Daniel remained at the court of the king.

The Fiery Furnace

Nebuchadnezzar was an egomaniac. He thought the world revolved around him. Even after Daniel's God had shown him his dream, he didn't change. In fact, he probably kept thinking of the golden head in the dream.

He decided he wanted more than the head. He wanted to be the whole thing!

So, he built a huge statue of gold of himself and set it in the plain of Dura, in the province of Babylon. Then he sent for all the high officials in his kingdom to come to Dura for the dedication of the image. That way they could all get a good look at how wonderful and mighty he was.

He had all kinds of musical instruments there. He commanded that when the officials heard the sound of the flutes, harps, etc. they were to fall down and worship the golden image. Anybody who did not fall down and worship the image was to be thrown into a burning, fiery furnace.

There were some Chaldeans there, who were jealous of the Hebrews. They saw and reported that Daniel's three friends, Shadrach, Meshach, and Abednego did not worship the golden image. They were Jews and they worshiped no one but God.

Nebuchadnezzar was furious! He commanded them to bring those three men to him. He gave them another chance to worship his golden image, but they refused.

They said, "We know that our God, whom we serve is able to deliver us from your hand, Oh King. But whether He does or if He doesn't, we still will not serve any other gods but Him."

That made Nebuchadnezzar really, really angry! He had them heat the furnace seven times hotter than it was before. He commanded his strongest men to tie up Shadrach, Meshach, and Abednego and throw them, completely dressed, into the furnace in front of him.

The furnace was so hot that it killed the soldiers who threw them in.

The three men fell down into the furnace, all tied up. But as Nebuchadnezzar watched, he saw their ropes burn off, and they got up and walked around in the middle of the fire. He couldn't believe his eyes. There was a fourth man with them in the fire who looked like the Son of God.

Nebuchadnezzar went as near to the fire as he dared, and called, "Shadrach, Meshach, Abednego, you servants of the most high God, come out of the fire!"

So the three men came out of the fire and went to the king. All the men around them had seen the same thing the king had seen, and knew they had been in the fire, but their clothes were not burned, their hair was not singed, and they didn't even smell like smoke!

Nebuchadnezzar said, "Blessed is the God of Shadrach, Meshach, and Abednego who has sent his angel and delivered his servants who trusted in him, and changed the king's words, because they trusted in him and would serve no other god."

Then the king decreed that nobody could say anything against the God of Shadrach, Meshach, and Abednego, because no other God could deliver his servants like their God did! Then he promoted Shadrach, Meshach, and Abednego in the province of Babylon.

Nebuchadnezzar's Dream

Nebuchadnezzar had another dream. This time he remembered it, but none of his wise men could tell him what it meant. Finally, Daniel came in. He told Daniel the dream and asked him what it meant.

When Daniel heard the dream, he hated to tell the king. He pondered over it for an hour. Finally, the king begged him to tell him, so Daniel did. But he told him that he wished it would be for his enemies, not for him.

Daniel told him, "God has decreed that Nebuchadnezzar will be out of his mind for seven years. He will eat grass and live with the beasts of the field until he recognizes that God is the one who made him ruler and gave him the place and power that he has. God is the one with the authority. But the kingdom will be given back to you when you come to realize that."

Daniel told him, "Leave off your sins, change your ways, show mercy to the poor; be kind and generous. Then, maybe God will not make this happen."

For a whole year, Nebuchadnezzar did what Daniel suggested, but then he forgot and reverted to his old self;

As he stood on the top of his palace and looked around, he began to tell himself how wonderful and powerful and majestic he was.

While he was still focused on giving all this glory to himself, he heard a voice telling him, "The kingdom is taken away from you until you know that it is the Most High God who really rules, and He gives kingdoms to whomever He wishes, and takes them away from whomever He wishes."

That same day Nebuchadnezzar lost his mind and was driven out of his kingdom. He lived outside with the animals. His hair grew long and shaggy like eagle feathers, and his fingernails became like bird claws.

At the end of the seven years, just as God had said in the dream, Nebuchadnezzar regained his sanity. He blessed the Most High God and praised and honored Him. Now he realized that God is the one in control.

From then on, he worshiped Daniel's God.

Daniel doesn't tell us anything about it, but it may have been Daniel who held the kingdom together during those seven years. If so, he probably reminded the officials that they knew what Nebuchadnezzar was like when he was angry, and they had best be doing their jobs because the king was coming back in seven years! Those who hadn't held his kingdom together would certainly be punished, but those who behaved well would be recognized and rewarded.

Belshazzar

Belshazzar was a successor or descendant of Nebuchadnezzar, and not a very smart one. He doesn't seem to have learned a thing from Nebuchadnezzar, who is called his "father," although he may actually have been his grandfather, or not even related.

Belshazzar had a banquet for all his noblemen and women in the palace, with a thousand people present. He ordered that the gold and silver dishes taken from the temple in Jerusalem be used. They drank wine from the dishes dedicated to God while they praised the gods of gold, silver, bronze, iron and stone.

Meanwhile, the army of Darius, the Mede, was outside, surrounding the city, but Belshazzar was so sure of himself that he paid no attention to it, and went ahead with his banquet.

While he and his many guests were praising the gods of gold and silver as they drank out of the temple vessels, suddenly a hand came out of nowhere, and began to write on the wall for all to see. It scared the king half to death, so much that his knees knocked together. It terrified all the noblemen with him, too.

He called for all the wise men to come in and tell him what the writing said. He promised that whoever could interpret it would be given scarlet clothes, a golden chain around his neck, and would be third ruler in the kingdom. But no one could tell him what it said.

Finally, the Queen Mother came in and told him how in the time of his father, Daniel had told Nebuchadnezzar the meaning of his dreams. She said for Belshazzar to call for Daniel, and he would tell him what he needed to know. So, he called for Daniel. The king acted as if he didn't know who Daniel was. When Daniel came, the king promised him all the things he had mentioned.

Daniel told him, "Keep all your gifts, or give them to somebody else, but I will tell you what the writing is. You know how God dealt with your father until he recognized that it is God who is in charge; but you, Belshazzar, though you knew all this, paid no attention. You have not listened to God at all. Now here you are, carelessly using the vessels from God's temple for your feast and debauchery, and praising the gods of gold and silver, as if they were something, when they can not see or hear or help you! So God sent you a message, using the hand. This is the message:

'MENE, MENE, TEKEL, PARSIN'

"It means: 'God has numbered your kingdom and finished it.'
'You are weighed in the balances, and found wanting.'
'Your kingdom is divided and given to the Medes and Persians.'"

Belshazzar commanded them to put scarlet robes on Daniel, a gold chain around his neck, and proclaimed him third ruler in the kingdom.

But that night Darius the Mede's army came through the water spouts under the city wall and Belshazzar was killed. Darius, the Mede, took the kingdom. God had finished Belshazzar's kingdom in a single night, just like He said.

The Lion's Den

Darius must have heard about Daniel's proclamation, because he appointed Daniel first ruler after himself in the new kingdom. He trusted Daniel and recognized the excellent spirit in him, even though he didn't understand how Daniel got his wisdom.

His other rulers did, though. They knew that three times a day Daniel went to his house, knelt in front of his windows that faced toward Jerusalem, and prayed loud prayers of thanksgiving and praise to his God.

These other rulers, presidents, and governors of the kingdom were very jealous. They put their heads together and plotted against Daniel.

They knew there was never anything bad they could say against Daniel. He was completely honest and trustworthy in everything he did. They had watched his life and the way he lived, for years.

They went to King Darius and sweet talked him into signing a decree according to the law of the Medes and the Persians that cannot be changed. The law said that anyone who asked for something from, or prayed to, any god but Darius, for thirty days, would be thrown into a den of lions.

Darius was a heathen and believed in many gods, but mostly in himself; so it was quite easy to convince him that he was a god to be worshipped.

When he heard the decree, Daniel went home, knelt in front of his windows as usual, and prayed three times a day, giving thanks to his God, just as before.

The men were lying in wait and they heard Daniel. They went to the king and reported him. Darius was furious with himself for falling for such a dumb thing. He knew it was for spite that they had done it.

He tried all night to get the law changed, but there was no legal way to get it done. The rulers waited for him and insisted that he carry out the law.

So, they took Daniel and threw him into the den of lions. Darius called to him, saying, "May your God, whom you serve continually, deliver you!" They put a stone over the top and left him all night. Darius didn't really believe God could save Daniel; he just hoped. He fasted all night and couldn't sleep. Very early the next morning, he went to the lion's den. In a hopeful voice, he called out to Daniel: "Oh, Daniel, servant of the living God, is your God, whom you serve continually, able to deliver you from the lions?'"

Daniel called back to him, "My God has sent an angel who has shut the lion's mouths so they have not hurt me, because I am innocent. I have not done any harm to anyone, and not to you, Oh king."

Darius was overjoyed that Daniel was alive. They took him out of the lion's den. They looked him over and found no hurt on him. Then the king commanded that those men who had plotted against

Daniel all be brought, along with their families, and thrown into the lion's den. The lions killed them all before they even hit the ground. As so often happens, the innocent suffered with the guilty.

THEN KING DARIUS WROTE TO ALL THE COUNTRY AROUND ABOUT AND TOLD THEM TO ALL FEAR BEFORE THE GOD OF DANIEL, WHO IS ABLE TO SAVE AND RESCUE HIS OWN FROM THE LION'S MOUTHS.

So, Daniel did well all during the reign of Darius, and the next king, Cyrus the Persian.

Who would have thought that a young teen snatched from his home of luxury, could be taken to a foreign country, made to live in their culture, could stand his ground for God so well that he influenced four pagan rulers to believe in his God, saved a kingdom for one of them, and changed all of their kingdoms for the better? One never knows what a teen can do when he follows God with his whole heart, like Daniel did!

DARE TO BE A DANIEL!

Daniel's Vision

Nebuchadnezzar had kept Daniel very busy and close to him all the time. Since Belshazzar hadn't really wanted Daniel around, Daniel had some extra time to think and pray to his God. God began to speak to Daniel in a new way. He gave Daniel his own dreams. Only they were more than dreams; they were visions.

Daniel realized from studying the scrolls of Jeremiah, the prophet, that the Israelites were to be captive in Babylon for seventy years. He determined in his heart to seek God and beg Him for mercy and ask Him to send the people back to their homeland at the end of the seventy years.

He started by completely identifying with the people and their sins and begging for God's mercy and forgiveness for all of them. He reminded God that only God is righteous. Others were all, from the greatest to the least, sinful people. He told God that it was not for their righteousness, but for God's own righteousness, that God should forgive them.

As Daniel was praying, the angel Gabriel came and talked to him. He said that he was sent to tell Daniel things because Daniel was greatly loved by God.

Daniel had another vision. He understood it was to be a long time in coming. He had been fasting and praying for three full weeks. During those three weeks, he gave up meat, wine and fancy food.

In this vision Daniel was standing beside the Tigris River. He looked, and he saw a man dressed in linen. His belt was made of finest gold. He glistened like chrysolite and his face appeared like lightning. His eyes were like lamps of fire, his arms and his feet like polished bronze; his voice was like the voice of a multitude.

Daniel said: "I, Daniel, was the only one to see him. The men who were with me began to shake and ran away to hide."

He said to me, "Don't be afraid, Daniel, because from the first day you set your heart to understand and began to pray and fast, your words were heard. I started out, but Satan's forces resisted me for twenty-one days, until Michael, a chief angel, came to help me. So now I have come to help you understand what will happen to your people in the future."

Daniel was told of other kingdoms that would come; how they would come; and who would rule in the future.

God's people whose names are written in His book will be delivered. The dead will rise; some to everlasting life and some to shame. The righteous will shine. Knowledge will increase. Many will come to the Lord. Many will not. Daniel would be long gone, but God's plans will happen in His time.

We are going to skip backwards in Bible history to a man named Jonah. We can learn a lot from Jonah. He's not a scoundrel, but he isn't a very good hero, either.

Jonah

Jonah was a prophet of the Lord. He was supposed to obey the Lord, his God. However, God gave him a job he didn't want to do. God told Jonah to go to Nineveh, a city of the Assyrians, his enemy, and tell them that God was going to destroy them if they did not repent.

Jonah rebelled. There was just no way he was willing to go to that wicked city of his enemy and tell them about his God! So, Jonah went down to the harbor and got passage on a ship heading for Tarshish. He was running from God and God's commands.

After the ship set sail, though, a great wind came up. It was so mighty that the ship was about to break apart. The sailors were scared silly. They told every man to pray to his god. They threw all the goods that weighted down the ship into the sea to make it lighter. But Jonah was sound asleep in the bottom of the ship; seemingly unconcerned that they were about to be swamped with the waves and drowned.

The sailors were very superstitious. They cast lots to see who was to blame for this terrible storm. The lot fell on Jonah. So they asked him to tell them who he was and what was the cause of this evil.

Jonah told them who he was and that he was running from the presence of the Lord, the God who created the world.

They asked him why he had done this and what could they do about it now, to save themselves?

Jonah told them to throw him into the sea and the sea would be calm. (Jonah would rather have been dead than to go and preach to Nineveh)!

The seamen didn't want to do it: but they were so afraid of dying, and of Jonah's God, that they threw Jonah into the sea.

As soon as they threw Jonah in, the sea quieted down. The men suddenly had a tremendous reverence for the Lord! They offered a sacrifice to Him and made vows. (So, Jonah inadvertently saved some foreigners, even in his rebellion).

Now God had known how Jonah would react to His command, so He had prepared a great fish. The fish came up and swallowed Jonah whole.

Jonah was in the belly of the fish, with water and slime and weeds wrapped around his head, and fish coming in every once in awhile; very miserable, but alive, for three days.

Finally Jonah called on the Lord. He begged Him to help him. He knew that the Lord had put him there for his disobedience. But he also knew the goodness of the Lord.

After three days of total misery, when Jonah finally prayed to God, the Lord sent the fish toward land, where it spit up Jonah onto dry ground.

What a boat ride!!

Then God repeated his order to Jonah, "Go to Nineveh, that great city, and preach to it what I told you."

So, Jonah got up and went to Nineveh. It took three days of walking to get across Nineveh because it was such a large city. He shouted his message, "God has said, unless you people repent, in forty days Nineveh will be destroyed!"

The people all repented of their sins. They put on sack cloth, and sprinkled ashes on their heads as a sign of their sorrow for their sins, from the king, down to the lowest person. The king made a decree commanding all the people to fast and pray, and everybody followed his direction. There was a great revival in the entire city.

But, instead of being happy for the change, Jonah was angry with God for it. He told God, "I knew you would change your mind and make me out to be a liar! I know how tender- hearted you are when people repent and ask for forgiveness. That is why I didn't want to come here in the first place!! Now, just let me die!"

Then Jonah went out of the city, and made himself a little shelter and sat in it. He was still hoping that God would destroy the city like he had predicted. He sat there and pouted. God made a vine grow up to shelter him from the sun. Jonah was very glad for the vine. It was too hot without it.

Then God made a worm kill the vine and it died. The sun beat down and a hot wind blew. Jonah was faint, hot and angry. Now he really wanted to die!

God spoke to Jonah and asked why he was so upset that the vine had died. "You didn't plant that vine or do anything to raise it," God told him. "It sprang up overnight and died overnight. You are concerned about a vine, but I am concerned about the city of Nineveh, where there are more than 120,000 children, besides livestock. So, when they repented, I spared them. Think about it!"

Our God is a gracious God who wants ALL of his children—everyone He ever made--to find Him and be saved; to serve Him and be able to enter the heaven that He's prepared for us. God has done everything needed for our salvation; but it is up to us to accept it.

If someone gives you a gift, it is not yours until you reach out and take it. God has voted for us. Satan has voted against us. Now it is up to us to make the deciding vote and choose our Master.

We have a choice.

Choose God!

Think about it!!

LaVergne, TN USA
19 February 2010
173598LV00003B/2/P